YOU ARE NOT ALONE

LEAH CUPPS

INKUBATOR
BOOKS

Published by Inkubator Books
www.inkubatorbooks.com

ISBN (eBook): 978-1-83756-391-3
ISBN (Paperback): 978-1-83756-392-0
ISBN (Hardback): 978-1-83756-393-7

PROLOGUE

A bitter, stiff wind blows off the lake, pierces my overcoat and chills me to my bones. It's been hours since the power went out. Montana is known for their brutal winters, but this year the drop in temperature came early. As I finger the thin shell of my coat, I realize I didn't prepare well for the weather.

I certainly wasn't prepared for this week.

A few hours ago, I could barely get a single bar of service on my cell phone. It was just enough to call 911. I've been huddled against the pillars of the dock, waiting for someone to come and rescue me ever since.

Now, a boat approaches cautiously, cutting through the frigid water. The light from the vessel splinters through the darkness, casting long silver threads across the water. The boat itself is cloaked in shadows, hiding the shape and identity of my rescuer. I should be relieved someone's finally coming, but I'm skeptical.

Lots of people have boats on the water. Maybe even some people I don't want to know I'm here. I purse my lips, trying to dispel the paranoid thoughts that have been dancing around my brain for the last few hours. My mind feels like a pressure cooker, ready to explode at any moment.

I wrap the papery coat tighter around my chest as I lean into the wind and peer into the darkness. Suddenly, the markings of a black and blue shield catch the moonlight. Another shiver runs through me as I confirm the boat's identity. It's the police, after all.

Finally, someone I can trust.

I lick the dryness from my chapped lips. Okay, *trust* might be a bit of a strong word. I still have a bit of explaining to do about my current situation.

I try to imagine the conversation I'm about to have with the authorities. How do I explain the two dead bodies that are lying inside the house behind me? Or how do I explain why there is blood all over my arm?

I rehearse the story again in my head. Everything, of course, happened by accident. People accidentally die all the time, right? I'm sure the police could tell me some stories.

Anyway, it was meant to be the perfect getaway with wine, hors d'oeuvres and a cozy hideaway on the lake. Sadly, the perfect getaway turned into a not so perfect and very messy set of murders.

But I won't mention any of that to the police. All they need to know is who did it. And I'll make sure and tell them *it wasn't me.*

PART I

NATALIE

1

THREE DAYS EARLIER

I glance over at my boyfriend, Hudson, as he speeds down the winding Montana road. His chiseled jawline is set in determination, but I can't ignore the nagging feeling that we may be lost. He may be perfect in every way, but he still has a few flaws. One of which is that he's terrible with directions. I finally break the silence.

"Are you sure we're going the right way?" I ask.

"Nat, I've told you a million times," he says, placing both hands on the wheel. "I know where I'm going."

I roll my eyes and look out the window. Natalie is my full name, but Hudson likes to call me Nat. It's supposed to be endearing, but it sort of irritates me. Sensing my frustration, he reaches over to touch my knee, which gives me a little jolt of pleasure. With coal black hair and light blue eyes, Hudson is strikingly handsome.

It was almost a year ago when we first met for a coffee date. At the behest of my friends, I put up my profile on one of those online dating apps. Hudson also had an account set up on *SwipeYes* and the algorithm immediately matched us.

When I messaged him, he said he was surprised and claimed he hadn't used the account in over a year. But once we started chatting online and I sent him a photo of myself, he said he had to meet me. When our eyes met across the café a few weeks later, it felt like destiny. I know it sounds cheesy, but it's true. We practically moved in together a month after our first meeting.

The two of us are weaving our way through the mountains en route to a secluded mansion on Flathead Lake. Hudson has planned the entire trip for us, down to the luxury BMW that smells like fresh pine trees. It's meant to be a few days of quiet romance, just the two of us. I've been looking forward to it for weeks.

A few of my girlfriends and I had drinks last night before we left. "Surely he means to propose!" they gushed as we sipped on martinis. I laughed off their comments. Surely he *should* propose.

I mean, not to brag, but I consider myself a catch.

I work hard to keep up my appearance. Between the grueling sweat sessions at the gym, the Botox, false lashes, acrylic nails and spray tans... I mean, I could go on. Let's just say I've turned myself into the personification of what men want. And in my business it's a must. You don't get far in real estate as a mousy, overweight brunette with glasses. Not to mention, dating in the twenty-first century is like a tightly packed horse race with no ribbons for second place. If you want to land a husband, you have to look just as good in person as you do on your over-filtered dating profile page.

So, like I said, I've done hard work to become the perfect woman. So Hudson *should* be offering me a proposal this week, but I have my doubts.

I look over at Hudson, who slows the car to let a small

family of elk pass. It's been nearly two hours since we left the airport. His lack of direction has gone from being slightly adorable to annoying.

I'm determined to play the supportive girlfriend, so I bite my lip and hold his hand instead of saying something about the fact that we were supposed to arrive at the cabin about an hour ago. The truth is, my stomach's growling and I'm ready to get something to eat and share a glass of wine over a crackling fire.

I fiddle with the black dial of the radio, looking for something to distract me from my growling stomach. There's not a lot of options out here, but I finally land on a local station.

"Today marks the one-year anniversary of the disappearance of Tess McDermott, a resident of Flathead Lake," says the radio host. We round another curve and the signal starts to fade. "The nation was captivated by the mysterious case and now..."

Hudson leans forward and turns down the radio. I glance over at him. "Tess McDermott... I feel like I've heard that name somewhere before. You know, I read somewhere that over 500,000 people go missing every year. Isn't that strange? I mean, where do they go?"

Hudson shrugs his shoulders, keeping his eyes trained on the road.

"We're almost out of gas," he announces. "I'm going to pull over up here."

I breathe the sigh of relief. Surely the gas station attendant can point us in the right direction. I mean, how big can this lake be? I pull out my phone while Hudson pumps the gas. According to Google, 197 square miles.

Great, we may never get there.

I crack the door and step outside, pretending to stretch

my back. Really I'm trying to get a look inside the convenience store.

"Honey, I see someone inside," I say, nodding towards the building. "Maybe you could ask for directions? You know, just to make sure we're on the right track?"

Hudson gives me a good-natured frown. "Fine," he says.

I slide back inside and relax back into my seat. I pull out my phone while I wait, periodically glancing up to see if Hudson is indeed getting us directions. To my dismay, there is no cell phone signal. *How do people survive out here?* A few minutes later, Hudson emerges wearing a triumphant smile.

"We're only fifteen minutes away," he says, plopping down into the driver's seat. "I told you I knew where we are."

"Right." I roll my eyes dramatically and give him a playful nudge.

Hudson showed me some pictures of the stunning Airbnb property we'll be staying at before we left. My jaw dropped when I saw it. Nestled on its own private island and surrounded by the clearest blue water I've ever seen was a massive stone mansion. My real estate brain was already calculating the value, which I was guessing was in the millions.

But what excites me the most is that we'll be far away from the city. This means that I will have my drop-dead gorgeous boyfriend all to myself. And sometimes that can be a little difficult. Hudson is a very successful executive for a medical device company, which means he travels a lot. Between his travel schedule and the long hours I work, we don't have as much time together as we would like.

Not to mention when we are together, both of us are guilty of constantly checking our phones. So I am excited for a few days of dodgy cell service coupled with a warm fire and fine wine. I picture us laughing, cooking delicious meals and making love.

Correction, *Hudson* is cooking us delicious meals. I'm afraid I can only manage burnt toast.

After some helpful instructions from the friendly fellow at the gas station, we arrive at the boat dock about twenty minutes later. I can hear the tires crunch over the gravel driveway as we approach a long wooden dock that stretches out over the lake. Two large stone columns flank the entrance and a metal plaque says Big Horn Manor.

Hudson jumps out of the car and runs over to open the door for me. I wait patiently inside the car, tucking a long red scarf around my neck. He's always been a gentleman.

I step out, and the two of us hold hands as we make our way to the boat. My heels are a bit unsteady on the gravel path, so I hold onto Hudson tightly. It's the middle of October, but the temperature in Montana has already dropped below forty degrees. I spent the last week planning the perfect fall outfit full of sweaters and cute jeans and boots, and of course, lingerie.

A man is standing at the dock, watching us approach. I assume he is the caretaker. He is tall, wearing a navy blue parka and a plaid wool cap. Hudson reaches out to shake the man's hand.

"Hello. I'm Hudson and this is my girlfriend Natalie," he says. The two men grasp hands.

"Welcome to Big Horn Manor. My name is Bart McKinney," he says with a Scottish lilt. I'm immediately charmed by the warmth of his voice.

"Please make yourselves comfortable on the boat while I retrieve your luggage." He tips his wool cap at us and heads to the rental car.

The two of us walk towards a gleaming wood boat, which bobs up and down in the water. It looks like it's about a hundred years old, although it's clearly been restored. Hopefully it's enough to get us to the island safely. From the stone dock entry to vintage style boat, everything about this experience so far feels first class. I lean in closer to Hudson.

It's clear he spared no expense to make our trip special.

As Hudson helps me down into my seat, I feel my phone vibrate in my pocket. I reach down and turn the phone on silent. It's probably my assistant Claire asking me another question about the big deal that we have closing a week after I get back from our trip.

Before I left, I explicitly stated that I should not be disturbed for a few days unless it was an emergency. Though I have doubts that Claire understands the concept of an emergency. One time, she barged into my office in a panic because the coffee machine wasn't working. I had to interrupt my call with a client just to guide her through fixing it. The thought alone makes me roll my eyes. I hope she can handle things while I'm away, otherwise what's the point of having an assistant?

Still, it takes everything in me not to reach down and pull open my phone. The deal we're working has been stressful to say the least. I broke a personal rule of mine, which is never invest my own money. But my partner Declan found a fantastic little apartment complex on the east side of Atlanta. As long as we can get the land rezoned, we'll more than double our investment. The only problem is the zoning commission has been giving us trouble. We're waiting to hear back from the committee, which means Claire may have some news.

"Do you need to get that?" Hudson leans in close and whispers in my ear, breaking me out of my thoughts.

"Oh, no," I say and push my phone deeper into my purse. *Claire can wait.* "Work-free week, right?"

He smiles and wraps his arm around me.

I lean into him. Hudson is my future. If my career doesn't work out, he has enough money to support us both. Another reason to love him. We snuggle into polished leather seats while Bart flips on the ignition. The boat's engine rumbles to life beneath us. I plant my hand on top of my wool fedora as Bart guides the boat out of the bay and onto the open water.

"I can't wait to spend the next few days with you," Hudson says. I turn my head so our eyes meet and lean in for a kiss. He runs his hand up my thigh. Another delightful zing runs through my body. I decide right then to pull out the lingerie I packed in my suitcase when we settle down for the night.

I hope Hudson enjoys the little surprises I have planned for him over the next few days. I wonder what surprises he might have in store for me.

2

"It's alright, honey, let it all out," says Hudson as he pats me on the back.

I'm currently retching over the side of the vintage wood boat. Not a great way to start a romantic getaway. I've been on enough cruises to know I get a little seasick over open water, but I figured since we'd be taking a short cruise on a flat, land-locked lake, I wouldn't need any medication.

I was wrong.

My ever-patient boyfriend holds back my hair as I continue to heave. I wasn't expecting such a choppy ride. All I can think about is getting to the dock and running to the bathroom to brush my teeth.

I'm sure Bart is a capable captain, but I still wonder if he could have chosen a smoother route. I read on the website that Flathead Lake is the largest lake west of the Mississippi, which might explain my current predicament. It feels more like an ocean than a lake. The boat sways again, and I grip my hand tighter around the railing. A brutally cold spray of water hits my face.

It's sunny in Montana, but don't let that fool you. The water is arctic-level cold. I was comfortable when we got out the car, but now that we are charging across the lake, I wish I would have dressed warmer. The cold wind seeps through every layer of clothing I'm wearing and sinks deep into my bones.

Raising my head, I try to focus on the stationary object in the distance. The island that we're heading towards. We motor around the large bay and a beautiful French-style house swings into view. Actually, I wouldn't even call it a house. It's more like a sprawling mansion, with multiple stone terraces cascading down the side of the island. The grandeur of the place is amplified by its size; it seems to stretch on endlessly across the plot of land. At the edge of the property lies a large dock, reaching out towards the chilly waters that surround the island.

As we get closer, the water seems to smooth out slightly, unwrapping the knots in my stomach. I'm able to pull myself back from the edge of the boat and settle into my seat.

"You folks still doing okay?" Bart turns back to face us.

I can't even open my mouth to speak as I'm trying to focus on taking a deep breath. Hudson speaks up for both of us.

"We'll be fine," he says.

Bart nods. "The house is right up ahead."

I peer ahead as the details of the massive stone-and-wood dock emerge from the water. There's a large boat house on one side, complete with a second story, and a few long rows of dock stretching out on the other. Again, my brain is making calculations on value, rows of zeroes floating around in my brain. If this place ever went up for sale, the agent would make a *fortune* in commissions.

Maybe I should hand Bart my business card on the way out.

"Almost there, folks. Hold on for a few more minutes!" Bart cries as he lines us up along one of the fingers of the dock. The boat slows to an idle and bobs up and down on the water.

As we pull in closer, a building surrounded by large pine trees comes into view. The grounds surrounding the estate are immaculate. Rows of manicured bushes and bright red and orange trees are set in perfect patterns around the large chateau. Hudson is squeezing my hand, but I can barely peel my eyes away from the house, salivating over the details.

He suddenly lets go and jumps up to help Bart with the ropes as the boat lines up against the dock. He seems very comfortable working around the boat. I make a mental note to ask him about his boating experience later.

Once we are securely tied up to the dock, Bart kills the engine. I gingerly make my way to the edge of the boat. Hudson jumps to my aid, reaching down to pull me up onto the dock. To my relief, the dock is unmoving and I feel my feet steady underneath me once again.

Bart appears at my side, offering me a warm wet cloth, a bottle of water and a cup of mouth wash. I must have looked surprised, because he smiles and says, "You're not the first customer to get a little seasick on the ride."

"Thank you," I muster. I eagerly chug the water and swish the Listerine in my mouth, before spitting it out in the lake. Luckily, Hudson is helping Bart pull up our bags, which gives me a moment to tidy myself up. I take a deep, cleansing breath and try to shift my mindset from seasick passenger to sexy girlfriend on a romantic getaway.

My gaze is drawn to the beautiful view of the shoreline

with its lush pine trees and colorful autumn leaves. I make a mental note to snap a photo to post on my Instagram. The property is lit up by a few scattered lights, and I imagine that would create a cozy atmosphere in the late afternoon sun. Although it's cloudy and there isn't much sunlight breaking through, the scenery is still breathtakingly stunning. I feel Hudson's arm wrap around my waist and I'm grateful for its warmth.

"So what do you think?" he says.

"It's beautiful."

Hudson presses a gentle kiss to my cheek before dropping his arm and striding towards the house with its massive oak doors reminiscent of a grand French chateau. The studded metal accents glint in the flickering light from the gas lanterns on either side and suddenly I feel like I'm sneaking through the back streets of Paris during the storming of the Bastille. I glance left and right, chilled to the bone.

Is someone watching me? According to Bart, no one else is here.

He walks up the entrance steps and flips open a wooden keypad cover and begins punching in a few numbers. I hear a strange noise coming from the trees down by the shoreline and turn to look over my shoulder.

Maybe an animal?

My eyes sweep around the landscaped property. A few birds flitter across the water, chasing each other into the wind. The trees continue to shake off their leaves, which flutter to the ground. A family of squirrels scurry by.

I shake my head. I'm being paranoid. No one is watching us. This place is like a postcard for fall in the mountains.

"Nat, are you coming?" says Hudson. I look up and realize he and Bart are now about twenty feet ahead of me.

"Yes!" I say, stumbling ahead.

I shake off the sense of foreboding and walk towards the door, taking Hudson's extended hand.

"As I said over the phone," Bart addresses Hudson, "the refrigerator is fully stocked with food and provisions, just as you requested. You should have enough to get you through the next three days until I return to pick you up."

Something about the idea that we'll be here for several days on an island with no way back to land suddenly feels unsettling. My palms start to sweat.

"What if we have an emergency? How would we get off the island?" I say.

Bart looks at me and cocks his head to the side. Hudson waves a dismissive hand at me.

"You'll have to excuse my girlfriend," he says, wrapping an arm around me. "She's a bit of a city girl."

My cheeks burn. *I can handle myself just fine.*

"Well, if you do run into any trouble, my lady," he points his head towards the water, "there is a small motorboat tied up to the docks that you can use to get back to shore."

I follow his gaze down to the docks, where a small metal motorboat is being tossed rather viciously up and down in the water. I blink a few times. With the turbulent waters that we've just endured to get here, I don't think there's any way I would survive a trip to the mainland in that little thing.

"But I will warn you," Bart says, looking us both in the eye. "It's a bit of a choppy ride. I would only attempt it if it's a real emergency."

I gulp. *That's exactly what I was thinking.*

As I glance at my luggage, I chide myself for packing too

much. Hudson's smirk earlier still lingers in my mind—he's right about me being a city girl through and through. Growing up poor was hard enough, and I wasn't exactly a girl scout. But in an effort to impress him, I've been pushing myself to be more adventurous. That's why I splurged two hundred dollars on the perfect hiking boots. A twinge of guilt washes over me, but I shake it off. This is all worth it if it means impressing Hudson and having a good time on this trip.

As Bart said, we have food, water, wine and of course, each other. And as I look at the house, I know we'll not exactly be roughing it. I imagine it's everything we need.

"Thank you, Bart, for everything," says Hudson, breaking through my thoughts. "We'll be in touch if we need anything."

Bart taps the tweed cap he's wearing. He turns on his heel and heads towards the dock. Hudson pushes the massive wood door open, and we step inside.

"Oh, folks, I forgot to tell you," Bart calls from down the hill. We both stop and turn. "There is a storm coming in this evening. Heavy rain, maybe some winds. The house has a generator. If the power goes out it'll kick in so you'll be fine." I look over at Hudson. He's watching Bart. "But just in case, the generator is located over on the far side of the property."

He points towards the west side of the island. "It's full of gas, but if you need anything just give me a call."

"Thanks again," says Hudson, waving him off.

With that he turns and walks back down to the boat docks.

A storm is coming in. *Great.*

3

W e slip off our shoes as we enter the house. Hudson takes my hand and leads me to a spacious living room. I assume that Bart came over early to prepare for our arrival, because a roaring fire casts a comforting warmth throughout the room. Any lingering thoughts of the storm begin to fade away. The air is tinged with the scent of pine and burning wood. Two large leather couches and plush chairs are arranged on a beautiful oriental rug in the center of the space.

This place oozes old money.

Sitting perfectly centered on the coffee table is a rustic wooden tray adorned with a tantalizing charcuterie board. Creamy, sharp cheeses are carefully arranged alongside clusters of roasted nuts and fresh, juicy fruits. It's like something out of a magazine.

My mouth waters when I see two glasses and a bottle of chilled champagne.

"This is amazing," I say, almost in a whisper. Hudson

grew up wealthy, so this must be normal for him. But for me? Even though I work in real estate, opulence like this still takes my breath away. It also makes me feel like a bit of an imposter. Like I don't belong here.

Hudson takes a few steps towards the table and picks up the bottle.

"It's already open," he says. He grabs the wine and pours it into two glasses. He hands one to me. Just as I am about to open my mouth, I notice a lipstick stain on the rim. I pause, furrowing my brow.

Good housekeepers must be hard to find around here.

I don't want to seem ungrateful, so I reach down and discreetly swipe a napkin from the table. When Hudson turns his back to walk towards the window, I quickly clean the rim.

"I can see storm clouds," he says as he looks out over the water.

"I'm sure it will be fine," I say, coming over to join him and rubbing his shoulder. "Let's explore the house and find our room."

"Sure," he says, turning to face me. "Oh, I forgot to toast."

He holds up his glass. "To a fun week." He gives me a mischievous smile as he wraps his arm around my waist. "And getting you naked."

I roll my eyes and smile.

"To us," I say. Our glasses clink and the two of us make eye contact while we take our first sip. As the wine slips down my throat, my heartbeat flutters. Hudson kisses me deeply.

Kissing a handsome man who adores me while staying in an uber-exclusive mansion is not what I imagined when I was slogging my way through community college. *But I could get used to this.* I feel a tug of desire for more than just a few days of hiking and great sex.

Hudson and I have been together for a year now. With his travel schedule it sometimes feels like about half that. But we have this connection that's hard to explain. We often spend late nights by the fire, talking about our dreams and what the future may be for us. He told me he loved me after we were together for only three months. So, maybe the girls were right about a proposal, after all.

Hudson leads the charge as we make our way towards the staircase. My phone buzzes in my pocket. I peel my jacket off and drop it on the one of the massive leather chairs. It's probably Claire again wanting to talk about the deal. But I've decided not to worry about that this week. Whatever happens with work, I can face it when I return.

I drain the last of my champagne, tipping the glass back until it's completely empty. We're now on the top floor of the house. There is a long hallway with bedroom doors flanking the sides. The first three bedrooms are nearly empty, each with a bed but no sheets or pillows. The fourth bedroom we enter is completely decked out in shades of blue, from the curtains to the throw pillows, to the bench at the end of the bed.

"I'm assuming this is the blue room. This is where Bart said we'll be staying," says Hudson as we peek inside. "I'll bring up our bags." He turns and bounds down the staircase, leaving me alone in the hallway.

I decide to skip the blue room for now and explore the rest of the third floor. At the end of the hall is a large set of double doors, and just like the front entry of the house, they scream handmade and expensive. I assume it's the owner's bedroom, which means it's probably locked. But I decide to give it a go regardless.

When I get closer, I realize that not only is the door unlocked, but it's slightly ajar. It's pretty much begging me to peek inside the room. I look over my shoulder to see if Hudson has made it back upstairs, before walking in.

The doors creak slightly as I move inside. I notice that it has been adorned in a similar style to the blue room. This room, however, is like a painting, perfectly composed, with every piece in its rightful place. The bed, a regal centerpiece, is meticulously made with crisp white linens and beige accents. There is also a dresser, a few nightstands, and some lamps scattered throughout the room.

Yet, underneath this surface perfection, I detect a hint of neglect and abandonment, like a dusty antique that has been forgotten in an attic. I step towards the large windows, which provide a stunning view of the lake. Part of me wishes we were staying in this room. But according to Hudson, the master is off limits.

I push open the door to the master bathroom, which is immediately to my left. Like the bedroom, it's over the top in its opulence, with expensive marble and champagne bronze fixtures. When I step onto the floor, I am surprised to feel the heat rising through my socks. Whoever the property owner is, they've spared no expense. It reminds me of some of the luxurious properties I've shown in the past, though this is probably worth millions more.

The master closet catches my attention. The doors are open, revealing a large two-story space with a glittering chandelier hanging from the center. As I walk inside I brush my hands along the clothes hanging neatly in color-coded rows along the walls. Cool silks and soft cashmere pass under my fingertips. Every brand of designer bag you can imagine is on display, from Chanel to Prada to Celine.

Whoever lives here certainly likes to shop. In fact, there's probably more money in this closet than I ever had in my savings account. *Especially now.*

The thought gives me a pinch of anxiety. I shake my head, pushing those thoughts aside. A strange thought crosses my mind. When we were in the car, the radio mentioned the missing girl, Tess McDermott, was a resident of Flathead Lake. Could this be her home? I pull my hand away from the racks of expensive clothes, a shiver running down my spine. What if these clothes belong to a missing woman? Or a dead woman.

Just as I turn to leave the room, a particular bag catches my eye. A green leather Gucci with a bamboo handle, just like the one... *It couldn't be.*

A few months ago, I was shopping with a friend at the Lenox Square, when I saw the most gorgeous purse ever. The color was a unique shade of green, sort of like the color of a ripe lime, but softer. When the store clerk saw me eyeing it, she informed me there was only one other like it in the States. I became instantly obsessed. I took a picture with it on my phone and posted it on the wall of my office. I promised myself as soon as I landed my next commission, I would return and buy it. About two weeks later, I sent my assistant Claire to the store to buy the bag, but when she returned, she informed me it had already sold.

But this bag in front of me? Looks exactly like it. I step forward and pick it up. The soft buttery leather feels amazing in my hands. I turn it over and notice how heavy it feels. Curious, I open up the bag. There is a leather-bound book inside.

I pull it out and set the bag back on the shelf. When I open the book, I see pages and pages of handwritten words. It's a diary. My heart flutters. Could this have belonged to the girl who went missing? If so, why is it still here and not with the police?

"Natalie?" Hudson's voice echoes from the hallway, startling me. I nearly drop the diary.

"Coming!" I yell back.

I make a quick decision. I pull off my scarf and tuck the diary inside, concealing it from view. Maybe I'll have time to read it later. If I find something important, I can tell Hudson about it and we can turn it over to the police.

Leaving the closet behind, I stride towards the bedroom door. As I close the doors behind me, I see my boyfriend carrying my three large and overstuffed suitcases down the hallway. He always goes out of his way to help me, and that's just one of the many reasons why I adore him.

"Here, let me help you, honey," I say, rushing to open the door for him.

"No, I got it, babe." He props the luggage against the wall and lets out a long sigh. "Where did you go?"

"Just the master bedroom at the end of the hall." I open up the top drawer and drop the scarf inside.

"Find anything interesting?"

"No," I say.

Just a little white lie.

I turn around to see Hudson giving me a peculiar look.

"Usually they have the owner's suite locked in an Airbnb. It's odd you were able to get in."

I shrug, not sure what to say. He approaches me from

across the room. It's not like I broke in. The door was unlocked. I chew the inside of my cheek. Maybe I should tell him about the diary…

"Are you feeling better? No more seasickness?" he says, rubbing me on the shoulder.

"Much better," I say. "Thanks for helping me out there. That was pretty rough."

Hudson leans in and starts kissing my neck. "I know something that would make you feel even better," he says, whispering in my ear.

Before I know it our lips are locked in a deep kiss, and Hudson starts to pull off my clothes. I get completely lost in the moment. Then from out of nowhere, I hear what sounds like a door slamming down the hallway. I pull away from Hudson, who is now without pants.

"Did you hear that?" I ask.

"Hear what?"

How could he not hear that?

"I thought I heard a door slam," I say, my heart beating faster. Hudson unsnaps my bra.

"It's probably from the wind. The storm is picking up outside," he says.

I look out the window and see dark clouds gathering in the sky.

"Should we close the curtains first?" I say.

"Why? No one else is here. It's just us," says Hudson, pulling me in closer.

Before I can object, Hudson takes off the rest of my clothes and the two of us are tangled inside the bed sheets.

AN HOUR LATER, we're still entwined on the soft bed. My fingers dance down his chiseled body, each muscle defined and sculpted from years of dedication to working out. His stomach grumbles.

"I'm starving," he says.

"Me too," I reply, brushing a hand against my own stomach.

He leans over and kisses me. "Why don't I go downstairs and start cooking dinner for us. You can take a long bath. Then we'll have dinner by the fire."

"By the fire sounds fantastic." The warmth from our cozy moment under the sheets has dissipated, and I'm starting to feel cold again.

A few moments later, I find myself alone. Despite my best efforts to resist the call of work this weekend, I cave and sneak a glance at my phone, only to be met with the cold, hard truth: no reception. *Probably for the best.*

I grab a robe from my suitcase and make my way to the bathroom. I study my reflection in the mirror. My makeup is a bit smeared but my blue eyes are still bright. I touch my roots, which seem to have grown darker since we left Atlanta. I swear, the older I get the more often I have to have my blonde highlights touched up. I make a mental note to call my hairdresser as soon as we return.

I switch my focus to the tray in the bathroom sink, which holds an array of luxurious bath products—salts, bubbles, lotions, you name it. I love these little touches. I pick up a few bottles and then decide to pour some bath salts into the tub. I turn on the faucet to fill it up.

As I walk back into the bedroom to fetch my razor, I remember the diary I discovered earlier. Retrieving it from my scarf, I run my hand over the cool leather cover.

Inside the first page is a handwritten title:

This diary belongs to Tess McDermott.

I figure I have about thirty minutes before Hudson expects me downstairs, so after I slip into the warm tub of water, I open the diary and begin to read.

4

Dear diary, or dear blank page...or whatever. I'm not sure whom I should be addressing this to.

I haven't kept a diary since I was a little girl, and honestly, it feels a bit silly. But my therapist, Dr. Sloan, has recommended that I keep a diary to help process my thoughts and feelings. So here I am, my first diary entry.

I never really thought I would be the type to keep a diary. I also never thought I would be the type to see a therapist either, but there's been a lot of changes happening in my life. First, my mother, who had been institutionalized for some psychological issues, passed away.

I hadn't really seen much of her for the last ten years. The institution she was staying in gave me the creeps. I managed to visit for Christmas and her birthday, but other than that I preferred to stay away. I told myself I wanted to remember her the way she used to be, back when I was younger and she wore makeup and expensive clothes... My mother was a knockout when she wanted to be. And besides, half the time I visited, lately more than half, she didn't even know who I was.

She suffered from early onset dementia. That's how the doctor described it to me. But to be honest? I always questioned my mom's sanity a little bit. She wasn't the most stable parental figure, mentally speaking. My father was never in the picture, so it was her and me from the start. After I turned six, things began to change. Mom stayed in her room, a lot. She would often forget to pick me up from school or piano lessons. I would sit there patiently, while my teacher would check her watch and make multiple phone calls on my behalf. It was humiliating at first, but I got used to it.

We lived in an enormous house with lots of bedrooms and bathrooms which had been decorated by some famous designer. As my mom's mental health deteriorated, she worried that everyone was trying to steal from her. She fired our maid and my nanny resigned, leaving only her and me to manage the household. The once pristine house became dirty and neglected, with an empty fridge and a growling emptiness in my stomach.

Boarding school was my saving grace. The strict schedule and rules were an adjustment at first, but without it, I don't think I would have survived. And for the most part, I turned out normal.

But I guess none of that matters now. She's gone to a 'better place', or at least that's what the priest told me. I'm not sure I even believe any of that.

After she passed, everything in my family's estate was left to me. I am the sole heir to what my lawyer calls a 'massive fortune'. He acted like I should be happy to inherit all this money, but honestly, I feel like it's more of a burden than anything else. Sure, I like the lifestyle it affords me, but I have no interest in carrying on the family legacy. Charity auctions, community center openings and galas are not my forte. I don't think the world needs another McDermott community center.

Not to mention the fact that as my mother told me many times, people will always be after your money.

This is where my psychologist tells me that my anxiety and paranoia kick in.

Even though my mother had a few screws loose, I think she was right. What people don't tell you about having a lot of money is that everybody wants a piece of it. Long-lost relatives, friends, boyfriends. Every single non-profit organization you've ever heard of has reached out to me since Mother passed away.

That's another problem. When Mother passed, my inheritance made headlines. The McDermott fortune caused something of a ripple in the news for a couple of months. In order to escape all the attention, I decided to come here to our secluded Montana estate on the island. It's really a lovely vacation property, but I feel extremely isolated, which only makes my paranoia and anxiety skyrocket.

The person I should trust completely is my fiancé, JJ. But even though I love him completely, sometimes I have my doubts about how much I should trust him. JJ and I have been together since we graduated college. Well, not the entire time. I did a little stint living in France for a few years, but we always kept in touch. But even after all the years I've known him, he still does it for me. And not just because he's drop-dead gorgeous and successful, but he's also good to me. When people ask me for money? He makes the call that I can't, the one where he tells them to leave me alone. He can also have a bit of a temper, but then I can too.

In summary, we're perfect together.

But sometimes I wonder if he loves me as much as I love him. He has to travel a lot for his job and sales, so I don't get to see him as much as I'd like. JJ's been really distracted with work lately. He says he's under a lot of pressure to grow the company so that he can get some equity. The way JJ always worries about his job and money makes me wonder if he too is with me just for the estate. Because I was an only child, sometimes I feel like it's hard for me to make friends, and so JJ is really the only one I have.

But I try not to think that way. I guess I wish he'd make me more of a priority. And maybe my mother passing away has made me a little more needy.

Anyway, JJ is coming to town this weekend. I am having Bart, our caretaker, bring in a full weekend of supplies. JJ loves champagne, so I have an entire case coming from our favorite winery in Napa. He'll be thrilled.

Well, I guess that's enough for the first entry. It doesn't feel so bad actually. Maybe Dr. Sloan was right.

5

Just as I am about to flip to the next diary entry, I hear Hudson's voice calling me from downstairs. My stomach rumbles at the thought of dinner being ready, and I quickly wrap a soft towel around my body before hurrying to get dressed.

After slipping on a warm sweater and sliding on a pair of delicate pearl earrings, I freshen up my hair and makeup. With a quick once-over in the mirror, I feel satisfied and reach out to open the diary once more. My eyes scan over the final pages, taking note of the precise handwriting and dark black ink that covers them. A reflection of her privileged upbringing and education, no doubt. A flicker of curiosity sparks within me.

She seemed so unstable. *Paranoid,* in her words. I mean, everyone has problems, but I always believed if you were rich, the problems wouldn't run as deep. Growing up poor I imagined all life's big problems were left to those who didn't have the money to solve them. Back problems from a lumpy bed? You buy a new mattress. Need a better job? Easy, you can afford an expensive education. Don't have enough friends? Those can be bought too.

But Tess's problems seemed to run deeper. I let out a long sigh. I guess you never know what happens behind closed doors.

I carefully wrap up the diary in my red scarf and stash it away in one of the empty dresser drawers, along with the rest of my clothing. I am not sure why I feel the need to hide the diary from Hudson. I'm sure that he would be interested in reading it too. But if he finds out I am snooping around, reading a missing woman's diary, then I will have officially broken our agreement to avoid any distractions this week.

I amble down the hallway to the grand staircase. As I take a few steps closer to dinner, I run my hands along the polished wood railing. The house is truly stunning. I would love to get a listing like this for my business.

I mean, who am I kidding? I'd love to *live* in a home like this. But unlike Tess, I didn't come from a large family fortune. I grew up with a single mother who was barely able to make ends meet working three jobs, including a third-shift position at a factory. Which means I barely saw her.

It was all she could do to scrape enough money together to send me to school. And college? Well, I managed to get an associate's degree from a local community college. But the job options where slim, so I eventually got my real estate license.

Once I graduated college, I promised myself I would never struggle financially the way my mother did. And I've done pretty well for myself. But money like this? It's something I've never even dreamed of having.

As I draw closer to the main floor, I can hear soft music. Hudson loves to listen to Frank Sinatra. He says it calms him.

I tiptoe the last few steps into the kitchen, hoping to catch a glimpse of him at work. When I do, I see Hudson standing by the stove with a dish towel draped over his shoulder, quietly humming to himself. The aroma of searing meat fills the air, mixed with the buttery scent of roasting potatoes.

"It smells fantastic in here," I say, walking up to him.

The kitchen itself is just as grand as the rest of the house, with a marble-topped island that's at least ten feet long. The hood over the range is made of stone and probably six feet wide. Even though Hudson is tall, he looks small standing in front of it. Hanging on each side of it are solid wood cabinets that were probably milled on site. That's how the rich think; everything has to be 'authentic'. Something I see every day in my line of work.

"What are we having this evening?" I ask, rubbing his back.

"I'm making us a couple of filets with roasted potatoes and green beans." Hudson gives me a sweet smile. Sinatra and a hot stove—that is his happy place. He told me once that his nanny taught him to cook, an idea I found otherworldly.

But even so, I find myself thinking what a wonderful father he would make. Cooking for us while the kids play in the backyard of our three-story brick-and-stone house in the suburbs. Naturally, I'd stay home after the second child arrived, given Hudson makes plenty of money to support us both. I'd probably pick up tennis and join a local book club. Our kids would have the best of everything; schools, clothes, sports, friends, colleges. If I did want to keep working, we could probably hire our own nanny. Of course, if he still had the same job he has now, he would never be home. But we have time to figure that out.

"I'll get the wine," I say.

"Great," says Hudson, barely looking up from his work. "Bart said something about a cellar in the basement. See if you can find us a good cabernet."

I head towards the staircase and unlatch the door that leads down into the basement. The air is cool and damp, carrying with it the earthy scent of soil and grass. As I descend, the sound of my footsteps echoes off the concrete walls, creating an eerie ambiance. I would use the term 'basement' loosely. The house appears to defy gravity as it clings to the island's steep hillside, each terrace seemingly carved into the earth itself.

Descending the stairs into the basement, I'm struck by the stark contrast to the rest of the house. The air is heavy with the musty smell of old books and animal fur. A few wall sconces cast a dim glow around the room, but it's still sort of difficult to see. Massive game animals adorn the walls, their glassy eyes following my every move. The ceiling is made of dark, polished wood paneling, giving the room an imposing and somber feel. Tucked in the far corner I can see a glass wall, and through it the outline of fitness equipment, a dumbbell rack and a full-size stuffed black bear. It is like stumbling into a taxidermy office masquerading as a living space.

I shiver. *I'm glad we're staying upstairs.*

After a few minutes of searching, I finally locate the wine cellar. It's a spacious room with rows upon rows of wine bottles. Bart never specified what we could or couldn't have, so I run my fingers over the dusty labels, trying to make a decision. I know just enough about wine to be dangerous. When I was in college, I waited tables at a local steak house. Part of our training included a monthly wine tasting. I didn't think much of wine then, but when I started dated Hudson, the knowledge came in handy.

I pick up several bottles and hold them up to the light, studying the color. I'm looking for something with a deep, rich color, and at least a three-year vintage. Probably from France, so it's spicy enough to pair with the steaks. After a few minutes, I find the perfect bottles and tuck them under my arm.

As I start walking back towards the stairs, I catch a movement out of the corner of my eye. An eerie feeling washes over me.

I take a deep breath to steady my nerves. *No one else is here.*

But just as I reach the staircase, a crashing sound comes from behind me, causing me to nearly drop the wine bottles. My heart races.

"Hello? Is someone there?"

Someone *or something* is definitely down here.

With trembling hands, I fumble with the overhead switches on the wall next to me. They flood the room with light. But even in the brightness, shadows seem to move and shift in the corners, the cold marble eyes of the animal heads staring at me.

Another noise echoes through the space, this time fainter but still distinct. My breath catches in my throat as I cautiously approach the wine cellar again. In a small alcove tucked away in the corner, I finally see what caused the commotion—a creature lurking in the darkness, its beady eyes fixed on me as I approach.

When I see it, I let out a sigh of relief.

"Well, hello, kitty," I say.

The cat stares at me for a moment, blinking her large

feline eyes. She has white cropped hair and green eyes. I feel her sizing me up. I slowly lean down and extend my hand. Finally, she comes up and rubs her back under my hand, purring loudly. I notice she's not wearing a collar.

"Well, aren't you a friendly little cat." I reach out and pet her. Since no one is living here, I wonder how she's eating. But the cat seems rather plump, so she must be good at catching mice.

"All right, little kitty. I have to head back upstairs." As I turn away, with the two bottles in hand, I feel myself relax. The strange feeling that we're being watched has haunted me since we arrived. That we're not alone. And this whole time, it's just been a cat.

As I work my way back to the main level, I feel my phone buzz in my pocket. I'd grabbed it when I left our room and brought it with me on impulse, intending to snap a couple of photos for my Instagram. My friends are going to be drooling over this place. Except for the basement. I'll probably leave that space out.

The reception here has been spotty since we arrived, but a message must have trickled through because my phone dings and alerts me of a voicemail. Wanting to listen to it before Hudson sees me, I stop at the top of the stairs and set down the bottles of wine. With a swipe, I open my phone and play the message.

"Natalie, it's Claire." Her voice quivers with urgency. "I need you to call me back right away. I just heard back from the zoning committee. I followed up with them earlier today and they said that no one called Declan ever reached out to them." There's a couple seconds of tense silence before she continues. "And I can't get hold of Declan. I think he's gone."

My grip tightens on the handrail. *She thinks he's gone? What the heck does that mean?* Panic wells up inside me. I want to dial her number and find out more, but I know Hudson would be furious if I break our pact. I bite my lip, trying to stay calm.

What did she mean by the zoning committee not hearing from Declan? He's my business partner, the one responsible for setting up this deal. He had found the perfect property and secured the necessary finances for us to obtain the loan. A sinking feeling settles in my stomach.

Granted, I've only known Declan for six months, but we've already completed two deals together. It seems impossible that he would just disappear without a trace...

"Natalie, there you are." I see Hudson come around the corner. "I wondered when you'd be coming back up with our wine."

I quickly pick up the bottles, caught off guard. He must have heard the voicemail playing on my phone. I need to come up with an excuse.

"Oh, yeah, just... I found a cat in the basement," I stammer, trying to recover. "That must have been what I heard earlier."

Hudson's mouth breaks into a wide smile. *Okay, he bought it.* My shoulders relax.

"See? Nothing to worry about," he says confidently, taking the bottles from my hands and kissing me on the cheek.

With a sigh of relief, I follow him into the dimly lit dining room. The scent of candles fills my nostrils, and I feel a flutter of hope in my chest. He pulls out a chair for me at a perfectly set table complete with wine glasses and a bouquet of roses.

"Roses? Wow, honey," I say, leaning in to give him a kiss before we sit down. "This is so thoughtful."

"Anything for you, Nat," he says with an endearing smile.

I should be over the moon, thoughts of diamond rings and white lace gowns dancing around in my head. But all I can think about is the fact that Claire couldn't get hold of Declan. In fact, she said he's gone.

And if Declan's gone? That means he's gone with every single penny I own.

6

A deafening crash shatters through the peaceful stillness of my deep sleep. Startled, I bolt upright in bed, heart pounding against my chest.

The darkness surrounding me is only briefly illuminated by a bright flash of lightning outside. Straining my eyes, I glance over at Hudson lying next to me, but he remains completely motionless, his breathing steady and gentle snores escaping his lips.

Did that come from inside or outside the house?

I hold my breath, listening to the relentless downpour that slams against the windows. Another loud clap of thunder shakes the room. I look over at Hudson, who hasn't moved. How does he sleep through all that? I let out a small snort. I mean, he's always been a heavy sleeper, but come on.

I instinctively reach out, ready to shake him out of his sleep. I pause. My mind is still adjusting to being awake, but even through the muddle an idea strikes me. Since Hudson is still asleep, I could use this opportunity to call Claire back.

Perhaps she has some news about the deal that she can share with me.

I pull my hand back, and gently peel back the covers. Still feeling groggy, I carefully get out of bed and fumble around for my phone. My hand wraps around it and I swing my legs over the side of the bed. Trying not to make any noise, I pull open the top drawer of the dresser and retrieve my scarf with the diary wrapped inside. Hudson stirs. I hold still for a few seconds. A moment later, he's snoring again.

Now equipped with my phone, diary, and scarf, I quietly make my way down to the main level of the house. The stairs creak ever so slightly. When I was a little girl I used to dream about living in a big house with a large spiral staircase like this one. We lived in a trailer park until I was ten, then my mom moved us to a small two-bedroom apartment near the factory where she worked in the suburbs. I used to lie in my tiny bed and imagine myself dressed in a sparkling silver prom dress with my hair swept up in an intricate updo. I would be stepping down the stairs, a big smile on my face, while a cute boy in a black tuxedo waited for me at the bottom with a bright pink corsage in his trembling hand.

Sadly, I never even went to prom. I was what you call a 'late bloomer'. A mouth full of braces, which my mom had to pull extra shifts to pay for, no boobs, and definitely no fancy clothes. Boys didn't really bother me, which suited me just fine. And no one asked me to prom. Even if they did, I couldn't have afforded a dress. So I spent my senior prom working my job as a pretzel maker at the local mall.

I'm sure rich girls have problems too, but at least all the ones in my high school went to prom. I push away the memory, putting all that behind me. I can make my own destiny now.

Once in the kitchen, I pull out my phone and dial Claire's number. Despite it being 3 a.m. here in the West, it's already 6 a.m. back home, so I assume she's up early, getting ready for work.

Claire isn't much for going out and usually works on the weekends. I would even go as far as to label her a recluse. I'm sure she gets asked out on dates. She's not unattractive. But she wears very little makeup, thick glasses, and her auburn hair is always slicked back into a tight bun. I've offered her the chance to join me and Hudson for drinks, or even a double date. But she always refuses, waving me off with a comment like how happy she is with her books and her cat.

I'm surprised when she doesn't pick up the phone. Maybe she's still asleep.

I bite my lip and plant my elbows on the cool marble kitchen island. I might try her again in a little bit. And now there's no way I can go back to sleep. I start to reflect on the deal that I struck up with Declan.

Declan had found a charming little apartment complex in a suburb on the outskirts of Atlanta. An old two-story, one-hundred-unit building that was just begging for a refresh. He told me that if we had the property redone and renovated, we could make a killing on the investment. So the two of us pulled together about a million dollars' worth of cash in order to secure a down payment for the loan.

Of that million, I invested about $500,000 of my own. Which is all the savings that I have. As soon as the loan closes, we plan to both pay ourselves out enough of a salary to cover us for the rest of the year. It is a must for me, otherwise I won't have enough money to pay my mortgage or my own bills.

I confided in Hudson about the deal over a glass of wine,

hoping for some support. But instead, he warned me against investing with Declan, saying he could get us both in trouble.

I disregarded Hudson's comments and told him to stick to medical sales and I would stick to real estate. The night ended in kind of a fight, and the two of us spent the night alone. Hudson went back to his apartment and I stayed in my own.

But the next day Hudson reached out to me and had flowers delivered to my office. He said he was sorry and that he adored me. He was leaving for a trip that day, but said as soon as we got back, he would make it up to me.

Now I'm wondering if Hudson was right.

Claire said on the phone that Declan was gone. What did she mean by gone?

It was Declan's responsibility to oversee the setup process. With his keen financial expertise and connections with the zoning committee, he managed to secure the majority of the approvals needed for the project. But Claire's message said that the zoning committee hadn't even heard of him.

I get a terrible sick feeling in my stomach. My mouth goes dry. There has to be a way to get hold of Claire. I need more information. Did she go to his office? Why does she think he's gone? I try her number again. And again.

Every time it goes to voicemail. Even worse, her voicemail box is full. *Great.*

I pick up my glass of water and take a long sip, feeling the cool liquid soothe my parched throat. As I gaze around the dimly lit room, I can't help but feel agitated. I need to distract myself before I go insane.

The diary. It's lying on the counter in front of me. I scoop it up in my hands and head to the couch in the living room. I flip through its pages, eager to lose myself in someone else's thoughts for a while. Maybe after some time with the diary, I'll try calling Claire again.

7

DIARY ENTRY #2 - JULY 15, 2023

Dear diary,
The last couple of months have been frustrating, to say the least. About a month ago, I was out for a run, making my usual loop around the island, which I've done a hundred times. And somehow I tripped over a rock I'd never seen before. When I fell, I used my left hand to try and catch myself.

Big mistake.

I could practically hear the bones of my wrist crunch when I hit the ground. After a visit to the hospital, I returned home with a fractured wrist and a cast.

You never really know how truly dependent you are on others until you lose the use of one arm. It's been depressing. I've stopped leaving the island and started having my groceries delivered. There's no point in going into town without my yoga as motivation. I told Dr. Sloan we had to do our weekly visits virtually.

Since JJ can't visit too often, he insisted on hiring a woman to help me cook, organize, and whatever else I need.

Her name is Francesca. She seems nice enough, but of course, I wonder what she's doing when she's going through my closet and all of my things.

I try to push those thoughts away. I don't want to turn into my mother, who was so paranoid that she couldn't let anybody even clean the house. JJ has come to visit a few times, but it's not enough. I miss him terribly. The couple of times he's been here have been okay, but we've gotten into a few arguments. To be honest, I am probably a little bit grumpy because of my wrist. The pain meds help, but they make my brain feel foggy.

JJ and I have been arguing about the wedding, and of course, the prenup. I'll be honest, talking about money with him makes me really uncomfortable, but I know it's necessary. The two of us sat down with John, my lawyer, who went over the terms of my trust. I did my best to try and read JJ's reaction when he found out that none of the money would pass down to him, but he seemed to take it just fine. Our arguments have been more about how we divvy up the properties we live on. JJ wants us to move to a house on the West Coast, where he's from. But he wants the house in his name.

Anyway, my arm is better now and the cast is off. JJ knew that I had been feeling isolated and suggested I invite some of my girlfriends out to the island for a fun weekend. I spent an excruciating week planning every detail, from hiring a massage therapist and nail specialist to arranging extravagant catered dinners for us.

I invited two college friends: Vivian Rockford, the wealthy daughter of a commercial property development mogul living in New York, and Monica Patterson, who recently got married and had a baby but is still struggling to shed the extra weight. Let's face it, Monica was never particularly attractive, her hair always a mess and her skin riddled with blemishes no matter how much makeup she slathered on. But at least she was still rather thin before motherhood took its toll. Vivian on the other hand was my college rival in every way, just as rich, skinny and pretty as me.

She and JJ were actually good friends in college, and I've accused them of hooking up more than once. But they both deny it. To this day they are still really good friends. Vivian assures me she has no interest in him.

Anyway, the weekend was a disaster. I tried to stay positive and spoil them, but it was never enough. Vivian complained about her lack of space for toiletries, while Monica was obsessing over her weight and refused to eat the expensive catered food. And then they both had the audacity to ask me for money—Vivian wanting an investment in some New York business venture and Monica begging for donations for her daughter's school.

I couldn't help but wonder if anyone wanted to spend time with me for anything other than my checkbook.

The only fun part was when Vivian fell into the lake. To be honest, I might have given her a little shove out of irritation. She wouldn't stop bragging about her designer bag and cashmere sweater, so seeing them stained with dirty lake water felt like poetic justice.

Once they left, I felt more alone and empty than ever before. Like my mother told me, you can't trust anyone when you have money. Except for maybe your lawyer. But with John, I have my doubts.

The only person I can trust is JJ. When he was in town this weekend, he brought me a surprise. A little kitten. I thought it was such a sweet gesture, and the kitten is pretty cute. I'm not an animal person but she's growing on me. I named her Gucci. She's rather needy but I've managed to keep her fed and given her plenty of milk. I refused to touch the kitty litter box so I let Francesca take care of it.

Did I mention I don't trust the housekeepers, either? Sure, they do a fine job, but I just feel like they're always looking through my things. In fact, I often keep my closet locked. I just have too many designer bags and heirloom jewelry in there for them to be tempted by.

JJ is coming into town next week so at least I have something to look forward to. I need to get off the island. I'm planning for us to have a little romantic dinner in town. Now that I'm off the pain meds for my wrist, I'm ready to get back to my yoga classes. Since I haven't been able to exercise, I've been drinking wine and watching true crime documentaries on Netflix. Dr. Sloan says this isn't really healthy for me given my paranoia. She's probably right.

But watching true crime shows just confirms what I already know. People are bad, evil even. And they'll stop at nothing to get their hands on what they want, especially if money is involved.

At least I have JJ. He's helped me so much. In fact, I'm going to talk to him this weekend about moving up the wedding. I think it's time we said our vows.

8

I want to keep reading the diary but I suddenly can't keep my eyes open for another second. With a deep sigh, I carefully push the diary in between the cushions of the couch. Maybe I'll have a chance to read more later.

The stillness of the house is only broken by the faint howling of the wind outside, rattling the windows. I take one last look at my phone before setting it on do not disturb. I yawn. I suppose whatever Claire has to tell me can wait until I get some sleep.

I make my way up the stairs and down the hallway, moving as quietly as possible. I hear a couple of thumps from the basement. My heart seizes for a moment. Being alone in this massive house at night is a little unsettling, but I take a deep breath and remind myself that Gucci, the resident cat, lives down there. Now that I know the cat's name, it somehow makes me feel less alone. I imagine Gucci stalking through the darkness of the basement, her sharp eyes fixed on any unsuspecting mice.

My footsteps fall like concrete on the top floor of the house. I barely have the energy to tiptoe to the bedroom door. My hand trembles slightly as I turn the doorknob, hoping to avoid waking Hudson. I peek my head inside. A small smile spreads across my face as I see his body outlined by moonlight, rising and falling with each breath. A twinge of jealousy courses through me; he always sleeps *so* peacefully.

Careful not to disturb him, I slip back the covers and then settle onto my side of the bed. As I close my eyes and let sleep wash over me, I find myself haunted by a question...

What happened to Tess McDermott?

———

THE FIRST RAYS of sunlight pour through the windows, casting a warm glow over the bedroom. The storm from last night has cleared, leaving behind a clear blue sky with only a few fluffy clouds floating lazily by. I reach for my phone to check the time. 8 a.m.

Stretching my limbs under the soft sheets, I sit up in bed and turn to look for Hudson. But his side of the bed is empty, marked by the imprint on the smooth sheets. I brush my hands over the place where he slept and feel cold sheets under my fingertips. He must have been up for a while.

Gathering my robe and slippers, I shuffle into the bathroom to brush my teeth and touch up my face and hair. A few moments later, I'm stepping into the hallway. The delicious smells of bacon and coffee hit me and my stomach growls with hunger. I can't stop myself from smiling at Hudson's thoughtfulness—he must have woken up early to make us breakfast. I wrap the robe around me tightly, trying to ward off the slight chill in the air. Perhaps Hudson can start a fire in the living room later.

"Good morning, sunshine," Hudson says. As I suspected, he has a full spread of ingredients laid out on the counter: eggs, bacon, some shredded cheese, and fresh herbs. "I made you breakfast."

"Thank you," I say, my eyes brushing the plate of eggs, bacon and a croissant sitting on the center island. I walk over to the coffee pot to pour myself a mug and then lean over his shoulder to watch him cook himself an omelet. Hudson turns to me and wiggles his hand inside my robe, brushing my backside. He smells of aftershave and a pine-scented body wash, likely from taking a shower before I woke up. I can't believe I slept through all that. Usually Hudson is the heavy sleeper, but this time, it was me who slept in.

I gently slide away. "Coffee first," I say, giving him a playful smile.

"So, how did you sleep, my love?"

"Okay," I say as I settle into one of the plush counter stools. "The storm woke me up a few times."

And then I snuck down to the living room, tried to call my assistant, and read a missing woman's diary in secret. But I don't mention any of that to Hudson.

"What storm?" he says.

I laugh. "I swear a bomb could go off and you would sleep through it."

He shrugs and points to my breakfast.

"Well, eat up, sleeping beauty, because we're going on a hike today. You'll need your energy." I smile and grab my fork as I settle down in front of the plate of food. The eggs are moist and fluffy and the bacon is cooked to just the right crispness. Hudson is a great cook, although he says he rarely gets the chance to hone his skills. He keeps a place in Chicago as his home base, but travels about three hundred days out of the year. So every time he comes to Atlanta, he either stays at a hotel or my place. Lately it's been more my place than anywhere else.

"I thought we could take the trails around the island and look for wildlife, like old married couples do," Hudson interjects while I'm mid-bite.

My heart pitter-patters as I swallow. *Old married couple? Could this mean a proposal?*

"Old? Who are you calling old?" I say, with a playful smile.

I devour all the eggs and a few bites of bacon, but I skip the croissant. As a soon-to-be bride, I need to watch my carb intake. Hudson is chattering away about his morning. Apparently, he got up at 6 a.m. for a run around the island and then showered.

I'm not much of a morning person. It's difficult for me to even form coherent sentences before I've had my coffee. After I finish the last of my bacon, I realize I left my phone upstairs. Glancing at the vintage-looking clock on the wall, I see it's already 9 a.m. here, meaning it's around midday at home. If I hurry, maybe I can catch Claire before she goes out for lunch.

"I'm going to run upstairs and change into my hiking clothes," I say.

"But before you do..." Hudson reaches over and unties my robe. His lips are on my neck.

"Here, really?"

"Why not," he says, his breath hot on my neck. "We're the only ones here."

My eyes flit around the kitchen. *So he says.*

But before I can give it another thought, Hudson pulls off my robe.

***

"You're amazing," Hudson says as we lean against each other on the kitchen island, breathless from our efforts. *We're amazing together,* I think.

It wouldn't have been my first choice of places to have sex, but I'm determined to be the super irresistible girlfriend he can't wait to marry. I wrap my robe around myself, coming back down to earth. We've lost some time, but I can still try Claire.

"I'm going to change," I say, making my way towards the stairs.

Hudson pulls on his hiking pants and reaches for a large newspaper that's folded on the corner of the island.

"Take your time," he says. "I found a paper on the dining room table. Bart must have left it. I haven't read a newspaper in years. I'm going to catch up on the local news and have a cup of coffee."

Closing the bedroom door with a soft click, I pad across the carpet and pull my clothes out from the dresser drawer. The familiar creak of the hinges echoes as I shut the bathroom door behind me and twist the lock.

I open the shower, which still smells of Hudson's soap, and turn the knob on full power. I hope the sound of running water will dampen the sound. With the water running, he definitely won't be able to hear me now.

I swipe open my contacts and press Claire's name. After three long rings, she finally answers.

"Natalie?" Her voice is filled with worry.

"Claire, it's me. I got your message. What's going on? What do you mean Declan is gone?"

"It's the strangest thing. I called the zoning committee like you asked and spoke to two different people there. Both of them said they had never heard of or spoken to Declan before. I was so confused."

My knuckles turn white from gripping the edge of the sink. I can see the nervous tremble of my fingers as they tighten and relax.

"I tried calling Declan multiple times, thinking maybe I had the wrong committee, but his number went to voicemail." She takes a deep breath. "So I went to his office. When I got there, it was empty. The desk was still there but all of his files and photos were gone."

There is a long pause on the other end of the line as Claire waits for me to respond. My brain is working at lightning speed, trying to make sense of this new information. I've heard rumors around the office about people being swindled by supposed investors.

A few years ago, Debbie, a seasoned agent of twenty years, was the envy of our office. She and her husband were on the brink of early retirement when a slick New York investor swooped in, promising big returns on local properties. With stars in their eyes and dollar signs dancing in their minds, Debbie and her husband poured half of their life savings into the opportunity. But just days before closing, the investor vanished into thin air, leaving the couple with nothing but shattered dreams and depleted bank accounts.

We watched helplessly as Debbie's world crumbled before our very eyes. She abandoned her career and started working in retail.

I couldn't help but feel a smug sense of superiority to

Debbie. Surely she hadn't done her due diligence. There must have been a line or two in the paperwork she missed or a phone call she didn't make. I figured with my street smarts, something like that would never happen to me.

Until now.

"Did he mention anything about switching locations?" Claire asks innocently, breaking the silence between us. Claire is completely out of her depth in this situation, but I can't blame her—no one could prepare for something like this.

"No, he didn't," I say, trying to sound more confident than I'm feeling. "Listen, Claire, everything's fine. I'll reach out to Declan on Monday and get things sorted out. In the meantime, could you email me a copy of the bank paperwork? I'd like to look over it again on the flight home."

I hear Claire let out a sigh of relief. "Of course."

"Enjoy the rest of your week. If anything else comes up, you can either call or text me. It's supposed to storm here all week, so my cell service may be a little spotty."

"Right," she says. "Thanks, Natalie. Enjoy your trip."

"Thanks," I say, then swipe my phone closed.

I stand there with the phone in my hand looking out the bathroom window. Declan is gone. His office is empty. And then the most terrifying thought of all crosses my mind.

He has all of my money.

I take a shaky breath and dial his number. As expected, the call immediately goes to voicemail. I call the number again, just in case. Nothing.

I shoot off a couple of text messages to Declan, praying that he'll respond. I make a mental checklist of all the ways I've contacted Declan in the past. He has a cell phone number, a local office number (now empty according to Claire) and a Gmail account. Let's face it, the list is short.

I keep my eyes glued to the screen, but with each passing minute, it's becoming clear that he won't respond.

The hiking clothes I packed sit neatly on the bathroom counter, catching my eye as a reminder of what I planned to do before all this drama with Declan started. No matter what happens with the deal, I can't let Hudson find out about the money. He explicitly told me not to work with Declan, and I didn't listen.

I twist my hair up into a bun and step in the shower. The hot water singes my skin as I try to regroup. After a few minutes, I step out, wrap a towel around myself and stare in the mirror.

How could I let this happen?

I choke down the rising panic in my throat with a glass of water. I check my phone one more time to see if any responses have come from Declan. I shake my head. The dread in my stomach is already telling me the truth. *I've been duped.*

I carefully apply some makeup and style my hair. I pull off the tags of my brand-new hiking gear and get dressed. I look every bit the part of an adventurous, attractive, soon-to-be fiancée.

Because if Declan really did steal all of my money? Hudson might be the only hope I have.

9

"Doesn't the air just feel cleaner out here?" Hudson calls back to me.

He's in a chipper mood today, and fortunately, the weather seems to match. There are still some clouds in the sky, but the sun is shining brightly. The storm must have already passed through.

While Hudson's spirits are lifted by the pleasant weather, I still feel like I'm under a dark cloud. I've been following him on our hike, gazing at the scenic views and navigating through trails and rocks. There is a mile-long loop around the island, which we have been working our way around for the last hour. I should be fully immersed in the moment, appreciating the skyline, birds soaring above us, and trees swaying in greeting.

But all I can think about is Claire's words. *His office was empty.* There was nothing left except a desk that came with the space.

Where the heck did Declan go?

It's hard to focus on the trail ahead when inside my

stomach is twisted in knots. That $500,000 is everything I have until my next commission. Which means I'll be living on my credit cards for the next two months until something comes in. I do a mental list of all my expenses, including everything from rent to my monthly fitness classes. I barely have enough room on my credit cards as is.

As I watch the broad shoulders of my boyfriend bob ahead of me, I know I can't say a word of this to him. Can you imagine marrying someone and inheriting all their debt? It would be an absolute non-starter. I feel like the proposal I hope to receive from him is already tenuous.

Don't get me wrong, I'm in love with Hudson for more than just his money. We have a special connection that I haven't felt with some of the other guys I've dated. And I know he loves me too. I'm just not sure if he loves me as much. It's the cruel fate of all couples: one always feels like they're playing catch-up in the game of love and devotion.

But given our age, and the fact that everyone I graduated college with has a baby or one on the way, I think it's enough for him to want to marry me. I've made sure to paint the perfect picture of a future for us. I'll give him his space to travel and play golf with his buddies, he'll give me the family I always dreamed of.

Which brings me back to the problem of Declan. If I don't find him and get the money back, I have nowhere else to go. I don't have any family to take me in. And I would never ask one of the girls from the office for a place to stay. Maybe I should apply for another credit card until I get things back on track.

My thoughts suddenly fall on Tess. She had money, and yet she worried everyone wanted to take it from her. Now it's possible I have none, and I wonder how I'm going to claw my way back. But unlike Tess, whose worries are merely hypothetical, my fears come with a harsh reality.

"You doing okay back there, hot stuff?" Hudson calls back to me.

I step up my stride until I've reached him. He's standing on the edge of a rock precipice, which juts out over the crystal-blue water. Despite the worries clouding my mind, I take a deep breath. I can't deny it. It is quite beautiful out here.

"You seem a little bit distracted this morning," he says, a look of concern flashing across his eyes. "Is everything okay?"

I have a brief moment where the words are on the edge of my lips. I could tell him—I could tell him all about what Claire told me—but it wouldn't help anything.

"I'm fine," I say. "I didn't sleep well last night, so I guess I'm just a little bit tired."

"Well, you'll sleep great after this hike," he says. "I figure we can do a couple more loops around the island and then have lunch. What do you think?"

I reach over and squeeze his hand. "Sounds great, babe," I say, giving him a tight smile.

I try to push down any thoughts of the deal and Claire and Declan as we continue our hike. I've always been in pretty good shape—not because of any natural talent, but because I work out at least six days a week. In my job, it helps to look your best. I'm not afraid to use my looks to my advantage whenever I can. So I'm surprised when I find myself slightly breathless as we climb up one of the steeper hills on the island.

When I arrive at the top, I stand next to Hudson. He reaches over and wraps his hand around mine, twining our fingers together. He turns to me. His hair is disheveled from the climb, but it's a good look on him. His blue jacket moves in the wind like a gentle wave. We stand facing each other, hands intertwined, like two pieces completing a puzzle.

"Natalie, there's something I want to talk to you about," he says.

My heart beats faster, almost fluttering with anticipation, as I feel the familiar stir in my stomach. I lick my lips in expectation. This is the moment I've been dreaming of, the culmination of our love story. He's going to get down on one knee and ask me to spend forever by his side. The air feels charged with electricity. Every sound seems amplified in this perfect moment. I can almost taste the sweetness of his words as they linger on the tip of his tongue.

"I know I've been traveling a lot for work. You've been so patient with me. And to be honest, the last year has been amazing. Every time I come to Atlanta, I feel like my life is complete. I love it there."

My mind is already picturing the giant rock he probably has tucked away in his jacket pocket. I can practically hear the tiny violin playing in the background, building up to this moment. With bated breath, I meet his gaze, inhaling sharply through my nose.

"So I have my place in Chicago, and I don't really spend much time there anymore." He takes a deep breath. "And I wanted to ask you..."

As I stand here, my arms quivering with excitement, everything around me seems to freeze in time. The crystal-blue waters of the lake sparkle and dance in the sunlight, while a gentle breeze ruffles through our hair, carrying with it the scent of fresh water and pine trees. I close my eyes and take a deep breath, trying to imprint every detail into my memory, knowing that this moment will be etched in my mind forever. The tranquil waters, the rustling leaves, the rich earthy smell of the lake. It's as if nature itself has paused to admire this perfect moment with me.

"Do you think I could sell my place in Chicago and move in with you?"

I stand frozen in place, my eyes wide and unblinking.

Move in together?

"What?" The word escapes my lips in a breathless whisper, barely audible.

Hudson's face transforms, his features contorting into a look of bewilderment. "I mean, I thought you'd want me to move in with you. Isn't that what you wanted?"

I press my lips tightly together, suppressing any words that may escape without my permission. My utter excitement over the expected proposal suddenly turns sour in my mouth. He wants to live together? At my little apartment in the suburbs.

You've got to be kidding me.

I don't want to give away a reaction just yet, but I can feel my eyes popping out of my head. I let go of one of his hands and take a step back.

"I don't know. I just thought you were going to..." I shake my head. "It's stupid."

I take another couple steps away, releasing his hands. Now he places his arms on my shoulders. "What is it? Is it too soon? Are you not ready for me to move in?"

Something inside of me snaps. I can't pinpoint exactly what triggers it—perhaps the pressure from dealing with both Declan and Claire, or the looming possibility of losing my apartment. But in that moment, I can no longer hold back. The words spill out of my mouth like a waterfall.

"I thought you were going to propose," I confess, my

voice echoing around the island. Embarrassment flushes my cheeks, even though there is no one else around to witness my vulnerability. It feels as if I have bared my soul to the entire population of Flathead Lake.

The wrinkles on Hudson's forehead deepen. He lets out a sharp breath and runs a hand through his dark hair.

"Oh, Natalie, I..." He's at a loss for words. I've left him speechless. The heat in my cheeks intensifies and runs down my neck. I should have never said that... Now he's going to feel obligated to propose, or worse, this will scare him away.

This is a disaster.

"I'm so sorry, I just..." He takes a breath. "I'm just not ready to get married."

Another thread of sanity snaps inside of me.

"You're not ready to get married!" I say, finally letting the flood of emotions open up. "How can you say that? We talk about our future together every night. How many kids we'll have. What our house will look like. Where we are going to live." The words keep coming even though the alarm bells in the saner side of my brain are going off. But I can't stop.

"We're in our thirties, for goodness' sake! How much longer are you planning on waiting to get married?"

Hudson now wears a horrified look on his face.

"Natalie, I'm sorry, it's just we're still getting to know each other. It's only been a year. There's still a lot we don't know about each other."

I stare at him. "I'm an open book," I say through tight lips.

Okay, that was a pretty bold lie... The deal with Declan...

But in that moment, I realize that he's probably right. It has only been a year, but with everything going on, I guess I didn't think about that. I was thinking about what I needed.

A partner. Someone who has my back. Someone who can help me out of this new mess I'm now in.

I scold myself for being so foolish. However, anger also bubbles up inside of me.

How could Hudson not have known the implications of his actions? Did he purposely mislead me into thinking he was going to propose?

"Whatever. It's fine," I say, turning away from him. "Let's just go back to the house."

The once clear blue sky above me becomes clogged with dark, looming clouds. They seem to be weighing down on me, mirroring my own troubled emotions.

We may have experienced a break in the weather this morning, but it looks like another storm is on its way.

10

Hudson and I hike back to the house in silence, with nothing but the sound of crashing waves and birds echoing around us. The clouds are huddling together now, choking out the sun. He glances back at me every few minutes, probably just to make sure I'm still here and haven't tumbled down the side of the island.

I'm still recovering from our conversation. I've not only broken but *shattered* the golden rule of dating: never make a man feel like he has to propose to you. It's supposed to be his decision, or else the proposal might never come. Never make a man feel like he needs to propose to you. It's supposed to be *his* idea.

Now, on top of the deal with Declan, I have another problem to solve. How am I going to patch things up with Hudson? I can only imagine that he's thinking the same thing right now. Is he considering breaking things off with me? Even though he loves me, he's made it clear that he's not ready for marriage yet.

Why?

I thought we had something special, something that neither of us have ever had before. But I guess I don't know much about his past. He said he's been in relationships before but I've never been one to pry. I figured he would just open up to me when he was ready.

A gust of wind suddenly blows against us as we reach the east side of the island. The rough ground scrapes against the soles of our shoes, sending small pebbles and dirt flying in every direction. The house is only twenty yards away from us now, but the path seems to end and curves towards the boathouse.

"Let's take a shortcut," Hudson's says as he points to a treacherous path of jagged rocks. My stomach turns in apprehension as I follow his gaze and bite back the urge to protest. I may be physically fit, but I am by no means an experienced hiker. The steep incline looks daunting.

Hudson watches me patiently, waiting for my response. Is this a test? Maybe by showing him how adventurous I am, he'll realize what an idiot he was for not proposing to me earlier. But who am I kidding? He probably just wants to get back to the house so he can call in Bart to take us home before the storm kicks up.

"Okay," I force out through clenched teeth, trying to mask my fear.

"I'll go first," says Hudson. He doesn't waste any time and leaps onto the rocks, carefully angling down the side of the hill. I watch him and admire his athleticism, which will hopefully be inherited by our kids someday.

Despite my reservations, I follow him closely, stepping cautiously on each rock as we make our way down the steep hill. But suddenly my foot slips from under me and I lose my balance. My body careens uncontrollably down the rocks, bouncing and tumbling like a rag doll before landing with a painful thud at the base of the hill.

Hudson rushes to my side.

"Nat, are you okay?" he asks, his eyes wide with concern.

I try to respond but find that my left arm is throbbing with pain. It must have caught on something during my fall. With a trembling hand, I reach over to touch the source of the pain. When I pull my hand back, I'm horrified to see my palm covered in blood. The sight makes me feel lightheaded and dizzy; dealing with blood has never been my forte.

When I was in college I decided to donate plasma for some extra cash. As I climbed down the steps of the donation center after the procedure, I suddenly felt woozy and disoriented. My vision blurred and everything went black as I passed out on the steps, leaving me with some ugly bruises.

I'm feeling the same way now.

Hudson seems to notice the blood at the same time. "Natalie, you're bleeding," he says. "Here, let me help."

Hudson quickly reaches for the bandana he has tucked in his pocket and applies pressure to my left arm, causing me to yelp in pain. The agony radiating through my body is blinding, and I fight to stay conscious as we make our way back along the path. Hudson seems to notice, because he bends down and sweeps me up in his arms.

As we pass the boathouse, I feel Hudson's grip loosen on my body. He seems to be struggling under my weight. I must feel like a ton of bricks in his arms.

"I can walk," I manage to gasp out, trying to ease his burden.

"Are you sure?" he asks with concern etched on his face.

I'm not entirely sure, but the thought of him dropping

me when I'm already in pain feels like a less appealing option. I manage to get a few steady steps under me, and then Hudson speaks up.

"Let's stop here and see if I can get inside the boathouse. Maybe there is a first aid kit inside," he says.

"Okay," I say, my voice sounding weak.

He walks to the front door and jiggles the handle.

"It's locked," he says. "We will have to try and make it to the house. Are you doing alright?"

I must be in shock, because the pain is suddenly less intense. I hold the bandana, which is now soaked in blood, on my arm.

"I can manage," I say.

Hudson's arm wraps around me with a steel grip, propelling me towards the house. I can barely focus on anything except the pain coursing through my body, but in the back of my mind, I notice the ominous dark clouds closing in. And then the rain starts.

It's as if the sky has been holding its breath, and finally, with a gasp, it exhales and a torrent of heavy rain drenches everything in its path. Including us.

As we toddle our way to the front door, my vision blurs from both the icy rain and my own agony. A flash of movement catches my attention—the cat, outside in the storm.

I try to form the words 'we need to let the cat inside,' but then I see something else. Someone else. A figure wearing a dark blue trench coat and plaid cap peering around the corner of the house. My heart races. *Is that Bart? He has a similar cap. But this person is much shorter...*

I try to tell Hudson, but I can't seem to get the words out. Suddenly the person is gone. I blink my eyes in the rain. *Was I imagining that?* My legs begin to wobble.

Hudson picks me up again and we make our way to the front door. My body is shaking like a leaf. I just want to lie down and close my eyes. Just as we arrive inside, a clap of thunder bellows in the distance.

It sounds like the storm Bart warned us about is back.

11

A few minutes later, I'm lying on the leather couch in the living room with my eyes closed, but I'm definitely awake. The sound of thunder reverberates through the air, pounding against the windows in powerful waves. My mouth feels dry and slightly metallic, likely a side effect of the adrenaline coursing through my veins after the injury.

My eyes flutter open. Hudson has laid a few towels down beneath my arm and used some kitchen dish towels to wrap up the wound tightly. He is sitting on the coffee table across from me, a look of concern engraved on his forehead.

"You're awake," he says and grabs my hand. "You had me worried."

I notice how clammy my hands feel. My hair is damp from the rain.

"I'm fine," I say, even though my arm is throbbing in pain. "I just don't do well with blood. It makes me faint."

Hudson reaches for a water glass next to his leg on the

coffee table. He thrusts a couple of white pills under my nose.

"Here, take these."

"What are they?"

"Just a few Tylenol I had packed in my bag," he says, holding them closer.

I lean forward slightly, causing another stab of pain to zoom up my arm.

"Have you got anything stronger?" I try to force a smile. Hudson shakes his head.

"I've looked all over the house for a first aid kit. I haven't been able to find anything." With his free hand, he reaches up and swipes a few raindrops from his forehead.

"This is all I have right now."

I attempt to adjust my position, but a sharp pain shoots through my body and I let out a groan. The discomfort is making me feel queasy. I fear taking any medication will only worsen my nausea.

"Can you make me a few pieces of toast? I'm feeling a little queasy. I need to get something in my stomach first."

"Of course," he says. Hudson jumps up from his perch and makes a beeline for the kitchen.

Now that he's gone, I breathe out a sigh. I'm trying to put on a brave face for him, but the truth is I'm in a lot of pain. Maybe he's right, maybe the Tylenol will help.

Twenty minutes ago I thought the botched wedding proposal was going to be the most painful part of this trip. I was definitely wrong.

I'm curious to see what's causing all this pain, so I suck the air through my teeth and gently pull away the dish towels. I immediately regret the decision. The gash running down my arm is at least five inches long and maybe half an inch wide. The way the skin is gaping open at the top makes me think it's not going to close up on its own. I start to see stars again. I quickly wrap the bandage back up, wincing in pain. If I look any longer, I might pass out.

Hudson returns, carrying a small plate with a few pieces of toast. He sits across from me again on the coffee table and offers to feed me the first bite. I take the bread from his hand.

"It's fine," I say with a brave smile. "I can manage to eat the toast."

Hudson looks a shade paler than he did this morning. His once perfectly styled hair is now drenched and darkened from the water. The intensity of his expression, filled with genuine and raw concern, makes me uneasy.

I'm not dying, I want to say.

As I nibble on the toast, I hear a loud clap of thunder. It rumbles through the house echoing along the tall walls.

"Is there anything else I can get you, Nat? Would you like some more water?"

"I'm fine, really," I say, swallowing down the last few bites of toast. I wash it down with a glass of water and the Tylenol pills.

As I catch Hudson's gaze, he shifts in his seat, leaning forward as if he has something to say. The fire crackles and dances in the stone fireplace, its warm glow throwing long shadows across his face.

"Nat," he says, pausing for a moment to rub his chin. "We need to go to a hospital."

I immediately shake my head.

"No, Hudson, it's fine," I say, although as soon as the words come out I realize that I'm probably wrong. It's *not* fine. I have a gaping wound on my arm that won't heal anytime soon. I think I just lost my life's savings and now my boyfriend thinks I'm desperate, which means he's probably going to break up with me...and then I'll be homeless...and...

My eyelids squeeze tight, trying to hold back the tears that threaten to spill over. The corners of my vision blur, but I refuse to let them fall.

"You're going to need stitches," he says, interrupting the spiral of thoughts that are threatening to overwhelm me.

I open my eyes again.

Stitches. Right. I just need stitches. I don't need to solve every single problem in my life right now. *Pull yourself together, Natalie.*

"I tried to call Bart," he continues. "The storm must've knocked out the cell phone service because I couldn't get through."

Bart. I think back to the figure I saw leaning against the corner of the house. "I thought I saw—" I shift my body weight, which causes a sharp stab of pain that runs up my arm. I cry out in agony. I shake my head again.

"I'm serious," he says. "We have to go for help. The boat is our only option. Remember what Bart said? If there's an emergency—"

"This isn't an emergency," I insist, through gritted teeth. "I'll be just fine. We just have to find a first aid kit."

"We need to take the boat back to the mainland," he continues. The very thought of jostling along the water in that rickety little metal boat nearly makes me want to throw up the toast I've just eaten. It was hard enough making it here when the sky was clear. But now? Now there's a storm raging outside and I've got a big gaping wound on my arm.

"You mean that tin can that barely floats?" I shake my head fiercely. "No way," I say, enunciating each syllable.

My shoulder and back are slightly squished against the couch, but I'm afraid to move again because the pain is so intense. I've made it clear to Hudson that there's no way we can get back on the boat. I take another sip of water. We sit in silence for a few seconds. The only sounds in the room are the crackling fire and waves of rain slapping against the house.

"We have to, Nat." He points to my arm. "That's not going to close up on its own. Without a first aid kit—"

"Wait," I cut him off, holding up my good hand. "Did you check the boat for a first aid kit? Most boats have one in the driver's box."

Hudson straightens his back. His eyes light up. "Nat, you're a genius. That's a great idea." He jumps up from his perch at the edge of the table and makes his way to the front door. I stare at the fireplace while he pulls on his jacket and shoes.

Then he comes back to stand over me, lightly placing a hand on my head.

"I'll go and check the boat. And maybe even the boat house again. It's locked, but if I have to break in, so be it." He leans down and kisses the top of my head. "Don't worry, Nat. I'm going to take care of you. I promise."

My shoulders relax. It's a good sign, the way he's caring for me. Maybe he won't dump me after all. Then I imagine him going back out into the rain. I remember the shadowy figure.

"I think I saw someone earlier, when we were coming back to the house."

"Who?"

I shake my head. "I don't know, but they were wearing a plaid cap, like the one Bart had on when he brought us here. Maybe it was him?"

Hudson frowns. "Why wouldn't he tell us if he was here?"

I tuck in my lower lip. He's right, it doesn't make sense. "I don't know. But when I looked again they were gone. I guess maybe I was just imagining things..."

Hudson reaches over and strokes my hair. "Listen, that was a rough fall and it was raining pretty hard out there. Don't worry about it. Is there anything I can get you before I go?"

I bite my lip thinking about how I might pass the time with the pain I'm in while he's gone. I imagine I must look like a wet clown, mascara and lipstick smeared across my face. I may be miserable, but I don't need to look that way.

"Would you mind getting my toiletry bag from upstairs?"

"Of course," he says and makes his way up to the bedroom. The pain in my arm has subsided slightly, enough for me to sit up. When I do, I feel a small lump in the couch.

The diary. I stashed it in the couch cushions before I went to bed last night.

Hudson returns and places the toiletry bag on the coffee table, just within arm's reach.

"I'll be back as soon as I can," he says.

After I hear the door click behind him, I grab my toiletry bag and touch up my makeup. It wasn't quite as bad as I thought and only takes me a moment to freshen it up. Since Hudson is gone and I have nothing else to do but feel sorry for myself, I decide to dive into the next entry of the diary.

Maybe Tess's mess of a life will distract me from my own.

12

DIARY ENTRY #3 - AUGUST 20, 2023

D ear diary,
      Yesterday was supposed to be the happiest day of my life. My wedding day.

But as I walked down the aisle, all I could see were the peonies and roses that seemed to mock me with their perfect blooms.

Because my wedding day was anything but perfect.

I stood there under a garish display of towering flowers, feeling suffocated and trapped in this elaborate wedding that some fancy New York wedding planner had put together. Was I building her resume or living out my dream wedding? It was the former, for sure.

But I wasn't about to back out, because I love JJ... and about fifty people were watching my every move. My lawyer, John, whom I hired because he has my best interests at heart, officiated the wedding.

As we exchanged vows, I couldn't help but feel like a puppet in this show put on for distant relatives and casual friends. Did anyone really care if I got my happily ever after?

Probably not. Like mine, JJ's parents died long ago so most of the guests watched from my side of the aisle.

My dress was one of a kind, flown in from New York and tailored to fit me by the designer herself. The weight of my mother's pearls around my neck brought both sadness and joy, a bittersweet reminder of her absence on my wedding day. JJ was every bit the handsome groom I always dreamed of. When he took my hand for the first dance, I even felt a small tear escape my eyes.

That's a pretty amazing feat, given the elaborate cocktail of anti-depressive medications Dr. Sloan has me on. She was there too, along with her doughy looking husband, who had a mouth full of petit-fours every time I saw him.

Vivian and Monica, two women who always have something to say about everything, were there, too. I welcomed them with open arms, lavishing them with compliments about their designer dresses and elegant sun hats. I managed to keep myself from shoving Vivian into the water again, but trust me, it crossed my mind a few times. I watched them from across the room, with their perfectly polished spouses, wondering what criticisms they were making about the event. Were they scoffing at my choice of a virginal white dress? Clearly I wasn't a virgin. Or perhaps rolling their eyes at the size of the flowers adorning each table? Even the finger foods were probably under their scrutiny, probably too dainty or not substantial enough. And, of course, the big question...how much did I spend? *Too much, undoubtedly.*

The white tents brought in by barge served as a stark reminder of just how far removed we were from reality. And I like it that way. Reality isn't always fun, and weddings are supposed to be about hope. But even though I felt like a fish out of water, I managed to put on the show everyone was expecting. No one truly cares about a wedding except for the bride. As long as there is enough money to throw an impressive party, people will show up.

In the end, it was everything I had hoped for on paper—magical and enchanting. But as we smashed cake into each other's faces and drank champagne by the bottle, I lost count of how many glasses JJ and I downed. By the time the guests left and the planner finished cleaning up, I was skunk-drunk.

And that's when it happened. The fight that tore through our perfect facade and exposed all the pent-up tension between us. The night ended in screaming and shattered glass, a far cry from the fairytale wedding we had just celebrated.

My worst fears were realized in that moment, and they came from the person I least expected—JJ. I made a tiny mistake by leaving the prenup paperwork lying on the dresser in our bedroom. My lawyer and I made some last-minute changes, which I had just signed that morning given the convenience of having a notary present.

JJ found the papers, and while I was changing in the bathroom, he managed to read the fine print. When I emerged from the bathroom, wearing only some lingerie, he was seething with anger over the prenup, his face twisted into a mask of rage.

I tried to reason with him, explaining that he wanted to know the contents of the prenup and I had told him the truth: that everything was set up in a trust for my benefit, with him being excluded in case of my passing. But he couldn't handle it. He couldn't fathom being cut off from the inheritance despite being my husband, bound to me until death.

As if dealing with everyone else asking for money wasn't enough, now JJ was joining in on the frenzy. My frustration boiled over and we got into a heated argument. In a moment of drunken rage, I slapped him across the face. The guilt weighs heavily on me now, but in that moment, all I could feel was anger and hurt.

I passed out after that, only to wake up at 4 a.m. replaying the fight and trying to engineer a solution. By the time JJ woke up in the morning, I had an idea.

Even though it was impossible for me to change the terms of the trust, I knew that I had the ability to set up a life insurance policy for JJ. And so I called my lawyer and made the arrangements.

Once JJ awoke, I had breakfast ready and waiting and the two of us sat down to eat. I told him about the insurance policy and how there would be $2 million waiting for him if anything ever happened to me.

JJ felt just as guilty as me, and was extremely apologetic. Things improved and let's just say the make-up sex made the fight almost worth it.

But now, the reason I'm writing this down in my journal? I can't stop thinking about the decision I made. Changing the terms of the life insurance policy seemed like a harmless gesture to make JJ happy, but now I realize it may have been a grave mistake.

I wasn't one hundred percent sure I could trust him before. But now? He has a reason now, a motive to want me dead.

My heart races when I think about families I've known that were torn apart by greed and money. The trust was set up for a reason—to prevent such chaos from tearing us apart.

Now, as JJ leaves for yet another work trip, I am left alone with my thoughts. The life insurance policy that I thought would make my husband happy now casts a dark shadow over our marriage. Trust has been shattered and replaced with suspicion.

As much as I try to push these thoughts away, they linger in my mind like a poison, consuming me. It's almost unbearable.

It might be time to make another call to Dr. Sloan and update my meds.

13

A loud crash echoes down the hall, jolting me out of my trance. My grip tightens on the diary as I hold my breath and strain to hear any other sounds. After a few tense moments, a meow breaks through the storm's roar.

It must be Gucci, Tess's cat. *How did she get out of the basement and into the house?* She saunters into the room, her fur wet and her almond-shaped eyes locking onto mine. She makes her way over to the couch and gently leaps on top. As she brushes against my leg, I tear my gaze away from the window.

How long have I been reading this diary? Did Hudson make it safely to the boathouse?

Gucci settles onto my lap. My arm is still throbbing but I manage to stretch out my good arm and give her a pat. She purrs.

I chew on my lip, thinking about what Tess wrote in her diary.

A motive to want me dead.

I really need to get this diary to the police. If JJ had something to do with her death, they need to know about it. In fact, she was concerned he was going to hurt her. Did the police know? Did they question him after her disappearance? I pull up my phone to do a quick Google search, but the cell signal is flickering in and out.

It's funny to think that twenty-four hours ago I was excited to have a break from my phone. I thought the dodgy cell service would be a good thing for me and Hudson. A few days without distractions. I couldn't have been more wrong. Being cut off from the world is never a good thing.

I shift my weight again, trying to find a position where my arm isn't pulsing with pain. I let out a long breath, looking around the room for something to distract me. As I do, I catch a dark shadow out of the corner of my eyes.

There are about six massive windows around the room that face the lake. When I look towards the south, I see the outline of a human figure standing just a few feet from the window, looking in. I can make out the silhouette of a trench coat and a wool cap.

I hold my breath. *Is that Bart? Or Hudson?* The figure looks too short to be either of them.

The storm has caused the clouds to go dark so I can't quite make out who it is. When I blink again, leaning forward, the figure is gone.

The sudden slam of the door startles me and causes Gucci to jump off my lap and run for cover. I quickly grab the diary and tuck it into the gap between the couch cushions.

"Hudson? Is that you?" I say. My heart is pounding as I wait for a response. Heavy footsteps against the thick wood floors come into the room.

"Natalie," I hear Hudson's voice.

My shoulders slump in relief. A moment later Hudson is standing over me, drops of rain splashing onto the floor. His clothes are completely soaked, outlining his strong shoulders. The shoulders of the person in the window were more narrow...but it had to be him. *Right?*

"Why were you looking in the window?"

He furrows his brow, and a confused look crosses his face.

"I wasn't. I came right to the front door."

My eyes flit to the window. *But I thought I saw...*

"Listen, Nat, I have good news." He pulls up a small plastic box with a large white cross on the side and flashes me a triumphant smile. "I found a first aid kit in the boat."

I abandon the idea of seeing someone in the window and focus on the box he's holding in his hand.

"That's great. Let's see what's inside," I say.

He opens up the case and starts rummaging through the contents. Hudson has mentioned before that he served as a lifeguard at his parents' country club. Hopefully that's enough experience to get us through what happens next.

"Here, look through this," he says, handing me a pamphlet titled 'First Aid Instruction Guide'. I flip through the pages, looking for anything on wound care. To my relief there is an entire section on large cuts like the one I've got on my arm.

Hudson glances over my shoulder. He points to the page.

"There, a section on stitches," he says.

My blood drains from my face, leaving a cold, clammy sensation. My stomach twists into knots as I struggle to maintain composure.

"S-stitches?" I stammer out, my voice barely above a whisper. "You want to stitch up my arm?"

"Yes," he replies with a calmness that only heightens my fear. He leans in closer, his eyes fixed on mine. "If we can stitch up your arm and stop the bleeding, we won't have to go to a hospital. We can wait out the storm until morning."

I understand his logic but...

"There is a stitching kit in the box," he says, fumbling through the pile of items on the table with shaky hands. "Here."

When I see the glint of a needle and thread, my vision blurs and I feel lightheaded. Hudson is studying me.

"Natalie, you okay?"

"Uh-huh."

His hand lands softly on my shoulder in an attempt to comfort me. Despite the pain, it works.

"Listen," he says, voice low and steady. "I think we can do this. I've been in the operating room at least a few hundred times, watching doctors stitch up their patients. We just need something to numb the pain."

The idea of Hudson stitching me up is enough to make my head spin. As a medical device rep, he regularly scrubs in for surgeries and trains doctors on how to use his equipment —I mean, I can only imagine the amount of time he spends in the operating room. So there's that. His lifeguard experience means he knows some basic first aid. But I highly doubt he was stitching people on the side of the country club pool.

He holds out a small tube of ointment. The label looks slightly worn. I stare at it, unsure if it will be enough to dull the pain.

"I don't think that's going to cut it," I say, feeling a lump form in my throat. I gulp for air, trying to push down the fear rising inside me, but it's hard not to panic at the idea of someone sewing my flesh back together while I watch.

"Maybe a shot of whiskey?" I suggest, half-jokingly.

Although I am not typically a fan of hard liquor, there were a couple wild nights in college where I indulged in a few shots of whiskey. Let's just say I don't remember feeling or seeing anything after that. So maybe a little shot of whiskey is just what I need right now.

Hudson seems to like my idea because he gives me a lopsided smile. "It's not a bad idea. Let me go see what I can find," he says.

He makes his way towards the kitchen, which has a small bar off to the side.

I look towards the window where I saw the figure in the trench coat and cap earlier. Maybe I am just imagining things. The pain and panic from being trapped on this island is going to my head. But it just seems like there is somebody else here...like someone is watching us.

14

"Got it!" Hudson announces triumphantly as he bounds back into the room mere seconds later, his enthusiasm practically tangible. Our eyes lock, and he flashes me a wide, confident smile. I muster a smile in return.

At least one of us is feeling good about this.

He plops down beside me, his energy still radiating off him in waves, and proceeds to pour me a shot of whiskey. I eye the glass warily for a moment, before downing it in one swift motion. The burn of the alcohol as it slides down my throat is a welcome distraction from the whirlwind of thoughts circulating in my mind.

"Another," I say.

He nods, pouring me another shot. I throw it back, embracing the fiery sensation as it scorches my throat, triggering a coughing fit that momentarily eclipses the pain in my arm.

"You alright?"

I give him a weak thumbs-up with my free hand. Hudson

pours himself a shot and gulps it down. His eyes settle onto mine.

"Ready?" he says.

I nod. I'm afraid if I speak, I might throw up the whiskey that's now burning down my throat. We sit in a tense silence, broken only by the howling of the wind outside. The storm is picking up strength, piercing through the sturdy walls of the house and making them feel as if they are swaying. The stone exterior may provide protection, but it does little to alleviate the unease that settles over us.

I feel a bead of sweat drip down my spine as Hudson prepares the needle. I clench my jaw, preparing myself for what's to come. As Hudson leans in with the needle, I grab the nearest pillow and bury my face in it.

I feel a painful zing as the needle pierces my skin. I let out a grunt, my entire body tensing against the pain. He pulls back and punctures my skin again. And again.

But despite the stabs of pain, it's not as bad as I thought it would be. The whiskey seems to be working its way through me, warming my belly and numbing my brain against what's happening.

Hudson's skilled hands continue to thread the needle through my skin, each new stitch bringing a pinch of pain. I squeeze the pillow until my knuckles turn white, trying to distract myself from what's happening. My palms are slick with sweat and my armpits are drenched as he works his way down my arm.

But then, suddenly, it's over. I hear the sound of scissors snipping the thread.

Hudson sits back and proclaims, "I think we did it."

Despite my trembling limbs and pounding heart, relief floods over me. I feel a slight pressure as Hudson wraps my arm in a bandage. I put down the pillow and force myself to loosen my jaw.

"Natalie?" he says. "Are you still with me?"

I finally turn my head towards him and look down. He's wrapped a clean white bandage around the wound and, to my relief, I actually do feel better.

"I'm okay," I say with a shaky voice. "I think... I think that helped."

Hudson lets out a long sigh. "I'm so proud of you, Nat," he says. He takes both sides of my face in his hands and kisses me on the lips. "You're tougher than I thought."

I manage a smile. He's right, I am tougher than I think. Tough enough to let my boyfriend stitch me up with a needle. And maybe, just maybe, tough enough to start over without Hudson's help, even if Declan has taken my entire life's savings.

As the adrenaline wears off and the danger is now behind us, every muscle in my body finally seems to relax. The exhaustion hits me like a wave, washing away any remaining resolve I have to stay strong.

"Thanks," I say, letting my breath out finally. "I am really tired."

Hudson stands up. He places a gentle hand on the top of my head. "Listen, why don't you take a little nap and I'll get dinner ready."

"Sounds perfect," I say, already settling back into the cushions of the couch. He grabs a blanket from one of the leather chairs and gently pulls it up to my chin. He places one last kiss on my forehead.

I close my eyes and let my mind wander. Within minutes, I am fast asleep, slipping into a dreamless sleep.

15

"There, how's that?" Hudson says as he ties a knot around my neck.

I woke up a few minutes ago to the sounds of Sinatra and the delicious smell of cooking wafting in from the kitchen. Hudson peeked around the corner and noticed I was awake. He quickly made his way to my side and fashioned my red scarf into a makeshift sling.

As he helps me up to my feet, I briefly consider telling him everything...it's all on the tip of my tongue. The failed real estate deal. My life savings gone. Declan's disappearance. And of course, the diary I've been secretly reading while he's gone.

But, maybe against my better judgement, I can't bring myself to do it. The whole accident and sewing up my arm... I can tell it's brought us closer together. Bonded us. Maybe it wasn't the trip I had in mind, but somehow I feel like maybe it's for the best after all.

Hudson takes my good arm and guides me into the dining room where he has set up a table for the two of us.

There are candles and what looks like a delicious chicken in mushroom butter sauce with green beans and roasted potatoes. I finally regain my appetite and take a deep breath.

I'm still a little wobbly, but I manage to settle down into my seat.

"This looks amazing," I say to Hudson. He smiles.

He pours himself a glass of wine, and offers me a one, but I shake my head. It's probably best that I not drink any more tonight. I need to keep a clear head, and honestly, wine doesn't even sound good after the enormous swigs of whiskey I had earlier.

Just as I take my first bite, the lights above us dim and flicker, casting dancing shadows across the room. The chandelier sways slightly, its iron chains creaking under the weight. Outside the window, the trees sway and bend in the fierce wind, their branches scraping against the glass.

Hudson and I look at each other.

"Didn't Bart say something about a back-up if the power goes out?" I ask.

Hudson continues to chew his food and then swallows.

"Yeah, he said there's a generator on the property. Nothing to worry about," he says.

Now that the emergency of my arm being injured is over, an uneasy silence falls between us. The urge to come clean about everything I've been hiding from Hudson bubbles up again.

"So, it's been quite an exciting trip so far," I begin.

Hudson takes a drink of his cabernet and chuckles. "You can say that again. You'll have lots to discuss with the girls over cocktails next week."

I wince at his comment, a bit of heat rising in my cheeks.

Yeah, like how you didn't propose. Hudson seems to notice my reaction.

"I didn't mean about..." he starts. I swallow hard.

"It's fine, Hudson, really," I say. The proposal is the last thing I want to talk about right now. Hudson takes a few bites of his food. "Actually, I wanted to ask you about something."

"What is that?"

"Did you see anyone when you walked down to the boat?"

Hudson gives me a confused look. "No, why?"

"It's just, since we arrived, I keep getting the feeling someone else is here on the island. And when you were gone, I could have sworn I saw someone looking in the window."

I study Hudson's face, waiting for a reaction. His expression reveals nothing.

"I promise you, Nat, it's just us here. No one else is on the island. I mean, take a look outside. How would they even get here?"

He has a point. Unless they were here before we arrived. But I keep this to myself. Hudson seems to have made up his mind. I hope he's right.

"You know what, I actually will have a little glass of wine. Maybe it'll help calm my nerves a bit. I'm still a bit shaken up from you stitching me up."

"Of course," he says, jumping up to grab me a glass from the kitchen. He lays a towel over his arm and makes a show of pouring me a glass. We laugh lightheartedly. Hudson returns to his seat.

"Thank you again for stitching me up," I say. "I am really grateful."

With my right hand, I reach across the table and grab his hand, which feels warm underneath my palm. "You take really good care of me," I say.

"Of course. I love you," he says.

"I love you too," I say. Maybe it's the wine or the feeling he gives me, but a warm sensation rolls over my body.

"So, how's work going?" he asks. "I haven't heard you mention anything about that big deal you've been working on with Declan. Any updates?"

I freeze, my fork suspended between the plate and my mouth. All the thoughts of the situation with Claire and Declan quickly flood back into my mind. I haven't even checked my phone since the hike this morning. Who knows if Declan or Claire have tried to reach me. I make a mental note to check my phone later, when the storm has passed and the signal is stronger, and see if Claire has any updates for me...

"Natalie, is everything okay? I seem to have lost you for a moment," Hudson says, interrupting my thoughts.

"Oh yeah, it's fine," I say, laying the fork back down. "We're just waiting to hear back from the zoning committee. You know, just politics."

Hudson leans back. "Tell me about it. I had this doctor last week who was dying to try out one of our spine instruments, but of course, he had to pass it by the board first..."

I relax into a comfortable stillness while Hudson entertains me with tales from his job. His voice has always been pleasant to my ears, deep and gentle, like a lullaby.

Hudson likes to talk about his work more than anything else. He once mentioned that his parents passed away when he was young, but he never went into much detail and I've never pressed him for more information. I'm sure eventually he'll open up about it in his own time.

It's a relief actually, because if Hudson shared his life story with me, then I might have to go into more detail about my own. Of course, I told him that I was raised by a single mother and that we struggled financially but made it. But he doesn't know about me living off peanut butter sandwiches or that I had to wear hand-me-down clothes or anything we could buy on sale day at Goodwill. He also doesn't know how much my friends relentlessly teased me for not having the latest clothes, shoes...latest anything. Not to mention the mouthful of shiny metal braces I wore, while they all had their dainty Invisalign retainers.

No, I didn't want to share any of that with my wealthy, well-to-do boyfriend because he'd just never understand what it's like to really struggle.

But all of that is in the past now. I am a successful investor and agent, and I can afford to buy my own designer bags and clothes. Just not as many as are filling up the closet in the upstairs bedroom.

"Well, I had an idea for after dinner," Hudson says, wiping up some sauce from his plate.

"What's that?" I ask.

"I found a cabinet with some board games inside. I thought we could play a few games and take our minds off things."

"Sure, that sounds great."

"I'll grab us another bottle of wine, and we can sit down in the living room," he says.

Hudson comes over and gingerly helps me from my seat. He walks me into the living room where I settle back into the couch across from the coffee table. He disappears into the kitchen and returns with a bottle of wine and a stack of games in his hands.

Operation, Monopoly, and Scrabble are stacked on top of each other.

"What would you like to play?" he asks.

"That's a tough one. Do you have a favorite?"

"Oh, Monopoly," he says confidently. "Monopoly is definitely my favorite."

I giggle at his choice of game. "I haven't played Monopoly since I was a kid."

"Yeah, me neither," he says. Hudson gets to work setting up the game on the table, carefully putting each piece in place. Of course, I only have one working arm, so I let him do all the work.

As Hudson lays out the game, I feel a little bud of hope blooming inside of me. He's been so incredibly sweet since I fell and sliced opened my arm. And then he braved the storm to look for a first aid kit for me and stitched me up so gently.

Maybe he's not ready to get married yet, but I'm pretty certain the man sitting across from me is definitely in love.

16

"You're really good at this," Hudson says, glaring at me but with a good-natured glint in his eye. We've been cruising through the game for about forty-five minutes, and in that time I've amassed three hotels and a slew of houses, including property on Park Place.

I shrug, a smile spreading across my face. "What can I say? Real estate is my thing."

My stomach clenches as I remember the deal with Declan. *Correction, was my thing.*

I reach over to place another hotel on one of my properties. Hudson's right, I'm on a roll. But as I study the loose strand of dark hair that falls over his forehead, I wonder if he's letting me win. I pull back and settle into the couch, bumping my injured arm in the process. The action sends a stab of uncomfortable pain up my injured arm.

"Ouch," I say.

Hudson's eyes flick up from his perch on the leather chair. "Are you okay? Do you need me to adjust your pillows?" he asks.

"I'm fine," I say, but I can't help but smile. Hudson has always been eager to help. It's sort of his personality—he's more of a giver than a taker, always willing to show his chivalrous side.

I think back to the first time he jumped to my aid. We'd only been dating a couple of months when I had a huge issue at work. One of the single-family flips that I was working on in the suburbs had a water leak. Scratch that, it was more like a water explosion.

In the middle of the night, a neighbor sent me a message saying that water was spewing from one of my house's windows. I remember being perplexed by the idea of water gushing out of a window, but nonetheless, I thanked him and hastily got out of bed. We had recently installed new drywall on the first floor, and any water damage would result in thousands of dollars in repairs.

Hudson was staying with me at the time, home from one of his work trips.

"Is everything okay?"

"Actually, no," I said, pulling on my boots and jacket as quickly as I could. "One of the water lines out of the property exploded. I've got to run out there and see what I can do."

"I'll come with you," Hudson said, already putting on his shoes.

I remember looking at him, perhaps with a bit of a skeptical face. My handsome, privileged boyfriend probably had little knowledge of basic household repairs like fixing a water line or a sink. But I kept my doubts to myself and gave him the opportunity to come along.

As we approached the property, it became clear that the

neighbor's warning was accurate—water was gushing out of a window. It was a chaotic scene, almost as if the very walls were crying tears of desperation.

With a flashlight in hand, Hudson managed to find the main water line within just a few minutes of arriving. With some effort and a wrench, he turned it off. Truthfully, I wouldn't have been able to turn off the water line on my own —it was almost sealed shut, with years and years of grime stuck to the outside. By the time the plumber had arrived, we had gotten most of the water out of the bathroom without damaging the drywall.

And that gave me a whole new level of respect for Hudson. He wasn't just some rich kid with an Ivy League degree; he was actually pretty self-sufficient.

I won't say that it was in that moment I fell in love with him, because that moment came long before. But it only added to the fact that I knew he was the one, the man of my dreams. Just as comfortable in a tux as he was with a wrench in his hand.

"All right, it looks like you have to pull a card from the Chance pile," he says.

I reach over with my good arm and draw a card from the deck. Before I flip it over, I give Hudson a sly smile.

"Any guesses on what it says?"

"Hmmm...maybe 'Go to Jail'?"

"Hey, that's not nice," I say playfully. He smiles.

But when I turn the card over, it's not a jail card or community tax. Instead, there is a handwritten note in bold, dark red marker. The message takes my breath away.

Declan's not coming back.

My cheeks flush with heat. A wave of shock rolls over me. Why would someone write on the card? How would they know I would pick it up? This feels all wrong. Someone here knows me, knows about the deal with Declan.

What the hell is happening?

I peel my eyes away to look across the table. Hudson studies my expression, a confused look on his face.

"What is it?"

"Oh, it looks like you were right," I say, recovering as quickly as I can. "I'm going to jail."

I take the card, flip it over, and do my best to slide it underneath the pile, unseen.

My heart pounds against my ribcage, the heavy thud echoing in my ears. It's obvious now, *we are not alone on this island.* And whoever else is here knows more about me than even my boyfriend does. They know about Declan. That he left. Which means whoever is here knows me. And from the way the card was written, this person is not a friend.

Panic sets in as I struggle to process this new information.

"Actually, you know what? I'm not feeling so great," I say with a shaky voice. "Would you mind if we headed to bed now?"

Hudson jumps up from his seat. "Of course," he says, wrapping an arm around me. "Listen, I'll help you get changed and into bed, and then I'll come down and clean up, okay?"

I nod gratefully. We stand up and he leads me towards the stairs. When we reach the edge of the room, I glance back over my shoulder at the colorful pile of cards scattered across the Monopoly board.

A sense of unease creeps over me. Who is on the island with us? How do they know about Declan? My heart beats faster as we near the top, and I can't shake the feeling that everything is about to change.

17

I wake up to the sound of thunder and a desperate need to pee. My hand fumbles for my phone on the nightstand, its bright screen illuminating the pitch-black room. The clock reads 3 a.m. The storm is still rumbling against the walls of the house and I can't believe how much it has rained in just the last twenty-four hours. I'm grateful that the house is perched on a hill. There's no chance that the water could rise this high.

Reaching for my red scarf, I wrap it loosely around my neck and wince as I adjust my arm sling. The injury still throbs painfully, but it's getting better.

I take a few steps and walk into the bathroom. I reach for the wall and flick on the light switch. Nothing happens. It's still dark in the room. I flip the switch again. Still nothing.

We're officially without power. Either the generator isn't working, or it doesn't power the whole house. I use the light from my phone to go to the restroom. As I sit there in the darkness, I think about the Chance card that I pulled tonight during Monopoly. And the note that was scribbled across it.

Declan's not coming back.

I was so shocked when I read it, I didn't know what to do. Hudson has no idea what's going on with our deal, and the handwriting was not his anyway, so I know it's not him. But if he finds out I've been lying to him? I'm not sure what he will think. But it won't be good. I just need more time to figure out what I'm going to do if Declan is really gone.

But the immediate question is: Who wrote that note on the card? And what are they doing here on the island?

I'm trying not to let panic seize control of me, but it's starting to sink in. We are not alone on this island. And whoever is here with us knows more about my life than my own boyfriend does. Not only that, but the way the words were scrawled angrily across the card, it felt like a theat.

I wrap the robe around my shoulders and make my way to the bedroom door. That gnawing feeling from earlier returns, as does a question...

Is someone stalking us on the island? If so, what do they want from us? Neither of us has brought much cash. I assume there's some expensive jewelry locked up somewhere in Tess's closet, but someone could just break in and take it. Why bother us? No, this feels more calculated, like a bigger plan is at play.

My thoughts wander back to the diary, which is still tucked between the couch cushions in the living room. Maybe there is some sort of clue inside that I missed. Something that will help shed light on the mysteries of this place.

I pause about halfway through the room. If someone is here in the house with us...I need something to protect myself. I peer around in the darkness. There are a few small accessories, some hefty pieces of furniture and a dresser full of clothes. *Not much in the way of weaponry here.* I grab a glass vase off the dresser. I feel a bit ridiculous, but at least it's something.

After I carefully close the door behind me, I make my way down the stairs using the light from my phone as a guide. As I tiptoe through the house, my thoughts drift back to how Declan and I originally met at an estate auction.

I took a seat among the crowd, my eyes scanning over the thirty or so people gathered around me. We were all vying for the same prize—a small property on the outskirts of Atlanta. Though it may not have been one of my most lucrative deals, I was confident in my knowledge of the area and in the skills of my trusted contractor who could renovate it in just thirty days.

The air crackled with anticipation as each bidder eagerly awaited their turn to make a play for the property. Let's face it, everyone in the room had the same idea as me. This was more than just a simple auction. It was a competition, and I was determined to come out on top.

After sixty minutes of tense negotiations, a man in his thirties with thick-rimmed glasses and an expensive suit snatched the property from my hands. I let out a sigh and began to gather my things. I stayed a few minutes longer and said hello to a few other agents in the room.

As I made my way towards the exit, I felt a tap on my shoulder.

"Excuse me, ma'am?"

I turned to see the man who'd just won the property.

"Yes?" I replied.

"I saw you were bidding on the Hickory Ridge parcel," he said.

"Yes," I said, putting my hand on my hip. "And I saw that you outbid me."

Even through his tortoiseshell glasses, I saw a look of amusement cross his eyes. He chuckled. "Well, I did do that," he said. I smiled and turned to leave. He stopped me.

"Listen, I'm new to this area. You know, the whole Atlanta market is kind of foreign to me. I actually was looking for a partner on this deal. Would you be open to grabbing a cup of coffee?"

I tilted my head to the side, sizing him up with a critical eye. His expensive suit may have been tailored to perfection, but it couldn't hide the slight wrinkles on his forehead or the tension in his jaw. He was nervous, and I was a sucker for a man who needed my help. Why not?

"Sure," I said. The two of us ended up going out for coffee that day. We spent a couple of hours discussing the deal. He was whip-smart and funny, which made me like him immediately. In the end, I partnered with him.

This was just the first of many business deals we had collaborated on in the past six months. Declan's work required frequent travel to the east coast, but he never went into detail about it. He did mention once that he used to be a lawyer, but I respected his privacy and didn't ask for more information.

Whenever he was in town, he generously provided the funds for any properties I found to flip. Our partnership had proven successful for both of us. I was able to save up a significant amount of money from the profits, and Declan had his own source of income to invest in our projects. I never pried or questioned where his funds came from.

About a month ago, he came to me with the apartment complex. It was the first deal where he actually asked me to contribute funds. A lot of funds. It was definitely out of my comfort zone, but I knew the area and I saw the potential.

Lots of young business professionals looking to work near downtown while keeping their commute short was a priority. We'd have full occupancy within a couple of months.

I trusted Declan, and the upsides of the deal outweighed any hesitation I might have had. Not only would we draw a monthly income from renters, but we could borrow money from the bank to pay us back until we sold the property three years later. On all accounts it was a home run. So, yeah, I wrote a check for my entire life savings.

I feel a knot tightening in my stomach. A decision I'm definitely regretting now.

Once I get to the bottom of the stairs, I make my way into the living room. I bring up my phone, which now has two bars of signal. Just enough. I dial Claire's number first. It goes to voicemail; no surprise there.

I try Declan's and, to my utter disappointment, it doesn't just go to voicemail. *The number you have dialed is no longer in service...*

The line says it's been disconnected. I feel like someone's just punched me in the gut. I set down the vase on the coffee table and slump down on the couch. I drop my head in my hand.

What am I going to do?

The truth hits me in the chest. *I need help.* If I ever needed Hudson's help, it's now. Maybe he won't marry me, but I know he won't abandon me either. I decide to tell him in the morning. The whole story about my investment with Declan, what Claire told me, the Chance card... all of it.

I adjust the sling around my neck, my arm still aching in pain. The house is quiet now save for the rain drumming against the windows. I reach into the couch cushions and a few seconds later the cool leather weight of the diary is in my hands. Using my phone as a light, I open up the next entry.

At the very least, maybe reading this diary will take my mind off the mess I've made of my life.

18

DIARY ENTRY #4 - SEPTEMBER 21, 2023

Dear diary,
Today has been difficult. It's one o'clock in the afternoon and I'm already on my second vodka gimlet. The sharp tang of citrus mixed with the bitter burn of alcohol is about the only thing that helps me relax.

Just for the record, I'm not an alcoholic...but I'm flirting with the idea.

JJ and I have only been married for a month, but it feels...longer. Our wedding was a blur of stress and tension, but we managed to salvage the celebration with a week in Tahiti for our honeymoon. Every day was filled with indulgence—extravagant meals, endless glasses of wine and cocktails, and passionate lovemaking. But even in paradise, the weight of our wedding night fight loomed over us like a dark cloud.

A silver lining? JJ was celebrating a promotion at work and he insisted on paying for everything himself. I think he was trying to prove to me that he didn't marry me for the money. I'm not completely convinced, but I appreciate his efforts.

Despite the temporary relief of Tahiti, I couldn't shake the feeling that our problems were far from over. I have decided to keep the life insurance policy in place...for now.

Since we've been back, JJ has been distracted. He tells me it's because of his new promotion at work but I feel like something else is going on. In fact, I worry that JJ might be cheating on me. It's hard to pinpoint why but he's on his phone all the time. And the other day when I pulled his phone out to check his text messages (don't judge), he had deleted his entire message history. Including the texts from me.

I thought that was...odd.

So the last few times he's returned from a work trip, I've been searching his suitcase for evidence. I feel a little bit guilty. JJ is a heavy sleeper so it's been pretty easy to access his luggage. While he's sleeping, I pull everything out and go through it meticulously in the middle of the night.

I've looked for all the usual signs: a smudge of red lipstick on a shirt collar, a secret message hidden in a pocket or the scent of perfume buried in the fibers of his jacket. I imagine I'll find a stray pair of women's underwear wedged between his neatly folded shirts. But every time I check his suitcase, I find nothing but a stack of business brochures.

But I know something is going on. *I can just feel it.*

I was too embarrassed to tell Dr. Sloan, so I turned to my lawyer, John, for help. I confessed my suspicions. John's father was a divorce lawyer, so he's heard it all. He didn't judge me in the least. He gave me the business card of a private investigator he uses on occasion, Sam Templeton.

I called Sam on the way home from John's office. He

happily accepted the job. That was two weeks ago. He's coming out to the island to meet with me today. He says he has news. Hence, the line-up of vodka gimlets I've been guzzling down.

I can hardly stand it. I know Sam's found something. Proof that JJ is cheating on me.

And if I'm right? There's not enough vodka in this whole town that will take that pain away.

19

A loud clap of thunder shakes the house, breaking me from my reading trance. I look up to see the light from outside illuminating through the frames of the window. It's definitely a little bit creepy down here by myself. I look back down at the diary. I only have one entry left. The answer to why Tess is missing could be on the next page.

Just as I turn the page, I hear the sound of glass shattering in the basement. My pulse quickens as I freeze, straining to hear any other noises in the stillness of the house. My body is tight and coiled, ready to react at any moment.

I suddenly long to be upstairs, snuggled up next to Hudson in bed. Just as I'm about to get up and scurry back upstairs, where my boyfriend can protect me, I hear footsteps echoing against the walls. I glance around the room, looking for anywhere I can hide. I grab the glass vase I took from the bedroom, ready to strike.

But before I have a chance to stash myself behind the curtains, I hear a familiar voice call my name.

"Nat? Is that you down there?"

Hudson. What a relief. Instinctively, I push the diary back beneath the couch cushions. I promised myself I would show him the diary tomorrow in the morning. Just not yet.

I stand up from the couch and turn to face him as he walks into the room. I shine my phone light towards him. His dark hair is sticking up every which way. He raises his hands to shield his eyes, which are half open, from the light.

"What are you doing down here?" he asks, squinting at me from across the room.

"I couldn't sleep, so I came down to get a glass of water," I say. What I don't tell him, of course, was how I came down to try calling Claire and Declan again on my phone. Or how I was reading Tess's diary. *Tomorrow,* I tell myself.

"Why are you holding that vase?"

"I'm trying to protect myself. I thought I heard someone, or something."

"Glass breaking?"

"I heard it too," I say. "It was downstairs in the basement."

Hudson makes his way across the room and wraps his arm around my shoulders. I suddenly feel more relaxed against his strong body. If anyone can protect me from whatever is going on in this house, it's him. After a few seconds, he steps away and walks towards the wall where the light switches are. He flips them up and down. "How long has the power been out?"

"I don't know," I say, shrugging my shoulders. "It's been like that since I came down here."

"Why don't I go downstairs and see if I can take a look at

the breaker box? Maybe then we could see where the sound of smashing glass came from."

I can't help but admire him; he's always thinking of a way to fix things. But as I stand there, watching him click the light switches on and off, a thought occurs to me.

"How do you know where the breaker box is?"

Hudson looks at me, a funny expression crossing his face. I can tell he's only half awake, but he still manages to mumble, "Bart told me that there was a breaker box in the basement. I scoped it out when we first got here."

I don't remember him ever going to the basement, but I shrug it off. "Okay," I say. "But I'm coming with you. If there's someone down there..."

He looks at me, his eyes suddenly awake. "Nat, it's just us, I promise. Didn't you say you saw a cat earlier?"

I nod. The cat has been the scapegoat for my theory since we got here. That cat sure makes a lot of noise...

"Then I'm sure that's what you heard. She's probably down there, hunting mice and squirrels."

I hope he's right. "Okay, but I'm still coming with you."

"Fine," he says. "Let's go to the kitchen and see if I can find a flashlight first."

I follow behind him, using the light from my phone to guide us. When we reach the kitchen, Hudson starts pulling open drawers one by one. Given the massive size of the space, it takes us a few minutes, but we finally find a flashlight in one of the island drawers. He flicks it on and a bright light circles the floor.

"It still works," he says, a look of relief crossing his face. I force a strained smile onto my face, hoping to reassure him as he turns to make his way down the dark, creaking staircase. I can already feel the hairs on the back of my neck standing on end, knowing all the dead, taxidermic eyes that await us in the basement.

As we descend, the air grows thicker and colder, like a damp blanket wrapping around us. A musty scent lingers in the room, a combination of old wood and aging animal skins. The beam of our flashlight illuminates the dusty floorboards and shelves lined with rows of lifeless eyes staring back at us. My heart races as I realize just how many animals have been stuffed and mounted in this eerie collection.

Note to self, taxidermy is not my thing.

A loud bang echoes through the basement, causing me to jump and grab onto Hudson's hand for support. Together, we move towards the source of the noise. My heart is pounding in my chest. This place is more than just creepy at night—it's downright terrifying.

"Hudson, did you hear—"

He turns and holds up his finger to his lips, calling for my silence. Gently clutching hands, we take a few more steps forward, our feet sinking into the plush carpet with each step. As we approach the source of sound, it begins to move. Sweat gathers under my arms.

A second later, Hudson's flashlight falls on Gucci, sitting in the corner of the room, her bright green eyes fixed on us.

"See, it's just the cat," he says with a smile, his voice low and soothing. He kneels down to the floor, extending his hand. She wastes no time in making her way towards him, her purr echoing through the quiet space. I kneel down next to him, watching Gucci's lean white shape rub against his leg.

"Wow, she really likes you," I say, studying the two of them.

"Yeah," he says, a strange look on his face. He reaches down and scratches under her chin.

"I never took you for a cat person."

"It's weird. She kind of looks like..." he says as her body rumbles with warmth. His voice trails off.

"Looks like what?"

He shakes his head. "Nothing."

He looks up at me. It's like he wants to tell me something, but then we hear a thud and a few of the lights flick on. Gucci skitters away into the darkness.

The flickering ceiling lights illuminate the room with a dim and unsettling glow, casting shadows across the walls and corners. The once-still taxidermy animals now seem to come alive, their frozen faces staring intently at us with their beady glass eyes.

"Looks like the generator kicked on after all," he says, looking around us. He runs a hand through his hair. "Well, I'm whipped. Let's head back upstairs and go to bed." He turns and gives me a teasing smile. "Unless you want to sleep down here with the animals?"

Just the thought sends a shiver up my arm. I playfully elbow him in the ribs.

"Very funny."

Hand in hand, we ascend the winding staircase, our footsteps echoing off the walls. By the time we reach the top, my chest rises and falls with each labored breath. I glance towards the living room as we pass, thinking of the diary tucked inside the couch.

There is just one entry left, but it will have to wait.

I follow Hudson into the room, slip under the covers and stay there, listening to the storm outside burst and rattle the windows.

A few minutes later, I'm fast asleep.

20

The next morning, I peel my eyes open. The storm continues to rumble in the distance. A muted, grey light filters through the blue velvet curtains, casting an eerie light around the room. I groan and try to sit up, but my body feels like lead. When I roll over and grab my phone, I see that it's already 10 a.m.

Great, I think, staring at the time, *I've practically slept the morning away.*

I look over at the sheets next to me and, to no surprise, Hudson is already gone. He probably got up and worked out in the fitness room in the basement. The thought of running amongst the dead animals gives me the creeps. Good for him though.

I lie there for a moment, staring at the ceiling. I promised myself that I would confess everything to Hudson this morning. The failed real estate deal, my empty savings account, the hidden diary. I take a deep breath, working up the courage to get out of bed.

I'm not looking forward to what I have to do.

I amble into the bathroom and splash some water on my face before brushing my teeth. Before I do my hair and makeup, I carefully peel away the wrapped bandage around my arm. And to my surprise, the stitches look neatly sewn together. Even though it's looking better it's still extremely puffy and sore. In fact, my whole arm is stiff.

I'm definitely going to need some more Tylenol.

I go to the side of the sink and find Hudson's toiletry bag. I rifle through the bag, looking for the white pill bottle labeled Tylenol. When I pull it out, Hudson's wallet falls out as well. His driver's license falls to the floor.

I pick it up and stare at his photo. My boyfriend is *so* handsome—but it's not his face that catches my attention. It's his name: Hudson J. Jenkins.

Seeing his name written down like this, I realize that, after all this time, I don't know his middle name. As I swallow the Tylenol pills with a gulp of water, it dawns on me that there are still so many things I don't know about Hudson. And unfortunately—or fortunately—there is a lot he doesn't know about me. I reach down for my mascara, flick some on my eyelashes and then stare at myself in the mirror. I've looked better. My hair is a bit greasy from not being washed and my under-eyes have a dark cast to them from the fitful sleep I've had the last few nights.

But I'm still there. Still pretty. Pretty enough maybe that Hudson will forgive me for lying to him.

I make my way down to the kitchen. It's still raining heavily outside. If there was any chance of this house being flooded, I'm sure it would have been by now. But the lake is so large, I guess it probably absorbs most of the water. The clouds from the storm keep the sky dark gray and gloomy.

With everything going on at home, I have to say, I'm a

little bit disappointed that our romantic getaway hasn't turned out any better. We still have a few nights left, but I seriously doubt there's a proposal coming my way, which means I only have about a day left before we fly home and I have to face reality.

The reality that all my money is probably gone. I know how men are, especially men like Hudson. They're looking for the perfect wife: beautiful, successful. Someone who will give their kids good genes and bounce back after pregnancy. Once Hudson finds out about my money troubles? It's probably going to be over.

Maybe I'm wrong. Perhaps I should be more optimistic and think that he really and truly deeply loves me. But time and experience tell me that I'm probably right.

I make it downstairs and walk into the kitchen. Hudson isn't there—he's probably still working out. I stride towards the coffee maker and pull out some fresh coffee beans and water, then pop them into the machine. A few minutes later, Hudson bounds into the kitchen.

"Well, good morning, sunshine," he says. He has a light sheen of sweat on his face, and I'm guessing he just came from the home gym. I can feel the heat from his workout and the sweet smell of sweat as he leans in to kiss me.

"I didn't know if you were ever going to wake up."

"I know, I can't believe I slept this long." I slump over the counter. "I guess I was probably exhausted from everything that happened yesterday."

"Well, you're much tougher than you look, I'll say that," he says, running his hand down my back and placing it on my behind.

"Why don't you have a seat and I'll whip you up some breakfast?" he says. I fill my mug with coffee and weave my way around the large island. Once I've settled into my seat, I take my first sips of coffee. It's strong, which is just what I need right now, *strength*.

"Is the power back on?" I ask.

"It's been touch and go," he says, running a hand through his hair. "Given we're on an island in the middle of a huge lake, I'm surprised we have any power at all. Right now, we've got power, but I'm not sure when it will go out again."

I take another sip of coffee. I pull out my phone and open it, hoping for anything—an email, a voicemail, a text message. Maybe a message from Declan saying the deal is a go and he was just out of town for a family emergency or something...

To my dismay, my message box is empty.

"Hey, Hudson," I say.

"Yes, my dear," he says as he whips eggs in a bowl.

"The girl that went missing, Tess McDermott," I say, in between sips of coffee. "Do you think this is her house?"

His hand pauses for a moment before transferring the eggs into a pan.

"It could be," he says. "I never asked Bart about the owner."

It has to be her house, I think. But I don't say it. "Do you ever wonder what happened to her? I mean, do you think she's dead?"

"I guess so," he says, continuing to make my breakfast. His back is turned to me, making it impossible to read his expression. "It's been a year and no one has seen or heard from her. They probably wouldn't be renting out this house if they thought she was alive."

He has a point. So that rules out Tess as the one who has been stalking us around the house these last few days. I guess this would be a good time for me to tell him about the diary. But I hesitate.

"Remember how I said I was able to get into the master bedroom?"

"Yes," he says.

"Well, there was a whole closet full of women's clothes in there. It looked like it belonged to her."

He turns around to drop a perfectly cooked omelet onto a plate. He places the omelet in front of me, along with a fork. His face is unreadable. "Bon appetit."

He seems content to drop the subject but I can't let it go. I should tell him about the diary I found. About her paranoia. But there is still one entry I haven't read yet. Maybe I can wait just a little longer.

I take a bite of my omelet, which is delicious. Hudson busies himself cleaning up the kitchen. "How's the arm?"

"Better," I say. "I took a few more Tylenol this morning to help with the pain. But it's manageable."

"That's great. Maybe I missed my calling as a surgeon?"

I laugh. "You did pretty well for a first-timer," I say.

As I finish the last few morsels of breakfast, I watch Hudson with admiration. He has a bit of stubble on his face, a dark lock of hair falling over his blue eyes. A folded dish towel is hanging over his left shoulder as he hums to himself.

You know you're in love when you think your boyfriend looks sexy washing dishes.

"Oh Hudson, I wanted to ask you something," I say.

"Hmm?"

"I saw your driver's license while I was getting out the Tylenol. Hudson J. Jenkins. What's the J stand for?"

My plate is now clear. He reaches over the island with a long arm and swipes it out from under me.

"My middle name? It's Jared," he says, adding another dish to the drying rack. "Actually, Jared used to be my first name. But I changed it to Hudson after college. Hudson was my mom's maiden name and it made me feel closer to her after she died."

"Has anyone ever called you JJ?"

He laughs, but there is a hint of unease in his eyes. "Only a few close friends used to call me that back in college. Why do you ask?"

The warm, bitter taste of coffee hits the back of my throat like a harsh slap. I nearly choke on it, coughing and sputtering as I struggle to get it out.

"You okay?" he asks, his big blue eyes filled with genuine concern as he looks up at me.

"Yeah," I manage to croak, still trying to catch my breath. "Just...coffee went down the wrong pipe."

JJ. Does that mean what I think it means? Suddenly, it feels like the only sound in the room is the rapid thumping of my heart, drowning out all other noises as my mind races with possibilities.

Was my boyfriend married to the missing woman, Tess? Has he been lying to me this whole time?

The questions are coming rapid-fire now, my mind drowning in the possibilities. He's never mentioned he was married before, but then, I never asked either. I can feel Hudson's eyes on me, but I keep focused on the mug of coffee, the steam warming my cheeks. I'm sure there are a million JJ's in the world, right? That travel a lot for work? That are in their mid-thirties?

And then a clear thought breaks through my panic.

I never finished the diary. But now, it has a whole new meaning. If Hudson is JJ and vice versa, then I need to know what the last entry said.

What did he do to Tess?

I need to get away, quickly.

"Do you mind if I head up the bathroom and take a bath? After yesterday—"

"Of course," he says without missing a beat. "I'm actually going to go outside to see if there's a better signal so I can try and get hold of Bart. I'm worried another storm surge and we'll have no power at all."

"Be careful," I say as he turns and walks towards the door.

But it's really not him I'm concerned about. *It's me.* If the man I've grown to trust is indeed the mysterious JJ from Tess's diary, a man capable of deceit and possibly violence, then I'm afraid of what might happen next.

A few seconds later the front door closes and I'm completely alone. I walk into the living room and slip my hand into the cushions of the couch to retrieve the diary. Book in hand, I trek up the stairs towards the bathroom.

A feeling of dread washes over me as I pry open the diary one more time. Because the pages I'm about to read could be the last written words of a dead woman.

21

DIARY ENTRY #5 - OCTOBER 1, 2023

Dear diary,

A few days ago, I met with Sam, the private investigator. I knew it wasn't good news as soon as I saw the look on his face. *I was right. JJ is cheating on me.* Sam brought me everything. The dates he was with her, the places they visited, and of course, photos.

The photos were the worst part. Sam's face was etched with a mix of pity and remorse as he handed over the envelope. Inside, there were images of JJ and another woman, lips locked and bodies pressed against each other. The photos hit me like a punch to the gut.

Sam brought other news. JJ's been lying to me about a few other parts of his life, too. But it's his infidelity I can't bear.

Somehow I held it together until Sam left.

Then I got piss-drunk and passed out in the kitchen. Francesca somehow dragged me up to my bed, where I stayed for the next few days, wondering what in the world I am going to do.

Of course, Dr. Sloan suggests I write out my feelings, so here goes...

I'm angry. Fuming, really. My blood is boiling in my veins, my heart pounding so hard I think it might burst. I'm horrified by what JJ has done. How could he betray me like this? After everything we have been through together, all the sacrifices I have made for him. I have given him everything, and this is how he repays me?

But what hurts the most is the broken trust. The deep, gnawing feeling of betrayal that consumes me. I thought I knew JJ, inside and out. I thought he knew me. But now, I don't know what to believe or whom to trust. Everything I thought I knew has been shattered.

The first couple of days Sam followed JJ, there wasn't anything suspicious. Routine meetings, lunches and surgeries with doctors. Then JJ traveled south to work in Atlanta. He visited one doctor's office and then headed to dinner with a woman on Friday night. This wasn't a working dinner; she wasn't a nurse or a doctor he was trying to impress.

No, she was a real estate agent. And a walking advertisement for plastic surgery. I couldn't escape the photos of her impossible, gravity-defying breasts, the too-tight dress from some bargain bin store, and the painfully obvious blonde highlights that screamed desperation. She may be deemed attractive by society's standards, but I could see right through her.

A gold-digging slut.

JJ had dinner with this woman at a nice restaurant downtown and then went back to her mediocre suburban apartment. Although the investigator couldn't capture them together in the room, it's clear that JJ spent the night there and left in the morning wearing the same clothes.

Which means he had sex with her. Just the thought of it fills me with nausea.

Initially, I thought it might have been a one-night stand or blowing off steam. Perhaps it wouldn't be unforgivable; maybe we could work through it. But then Sam revealed that he has been seeing her almost every night during his travels. Between client visits, they go out for lunch, visit the zoo, and indulge in these little romantic excursions. I can hardly believe it—the audacity of this bimbo who stole my husband.

When JJ returned home yesterday, I confronted him about his infidelity. The lies rolled off his tongue like poison, denying any wrongdoing with ease. In that moment, something inside me snapped. The man in front of me is not who I thought I married. I realized he has probably been using me all along for my wealth and status.

Our argument became heated, and JJ became violent. I'll admit I struck him first, but when he slapped me across the face, the look in his eyes resembled that of a monster. Now I fear for my life.

Why? *The life insurance policy.* The one I signed the morning after our wedding to make my husband happy. To let him know I trusted him. We haven't spoken about it since our wedding night, but it's still there, looming over us like a dark cloud.

JJ managed to calm me down after the fight. He has a knack for twisting my thoughts and making me doubt my own sanity. I ended up falling asleep in his arms last night.

But this morning, everything has come crashing back with the harsh reality of the morning light. *And I am worried.*

JJ planned a romantic boat tour of the Flathead Lake today. Just the two of us. He's packing us a full lunch with a few bottles of wine. He told me there's a little island about a half hour from here where we can have a picnic. He said we can talk more about what happened, work things out.

But in truth, I'm afraid.

I'm afraid that once we get out on the big open water, he'll turn against me. No one would hear me scream; the lake is huge. And no one would see if he decided to tie an anchor around my waist and dump my lifeless body in the water.

So if you're reading this diary and I've gone missing, it means I'm dead. Give my diary to the police. And make sure and tell them who killed me.

Hudson Jared Jenkins.

22

I fling the diary to the ground as if it's a ticking time bomb. My heart feels like it's about to burst through my chest, each beat thundering in my ears. I stagger back against the hard porcelain of the tub, my fingers clawing at its smooth surface for support. The storm outside unleashes its fury, pounding against the windows with a deafening roar.

My mind is reeling, frantically trying to process the bombshell revelations written on those pages. Each word hits me like a physical blow, knocking the air out of my lungs and leaving me gasping for breath.

Hudson was married to Tess McDermott.

He lied to me about knowing who she was. And about this house. It's his house!

He cheated on his wife, with me.

She claims he killed her.

The words cut like shards of glass, each one hitting its mark with brutal precision.

"Real estate bimbo from Atlanta." Tess's cruel words

linger in my mind as I feel the weight of her judgement crushing me. But can I really blame her? I was unknowingly involved in an affair with a married man, and now I'm left wondering if he could be capable of murder.

I stare at the journal on the cold bathroom floor, its pages filled with damning evidence against Hudson. A year ago, Tess's voice spilled out onto these very pages, detailing his manipulations and lies. Did he do it? Did he kill her for the money?

My head spins. How did I not see the signs? How could I have been so blind? With shaking hands, I pick up the diary off the floor and place it on the counter, staring at its cover.

What am I going to do now?

My options are pretty limited. Yes, there is a boat tied down to the docks. But given the storm raging outside, I'd probably drown before I made it to land. That's if I didn't pass out from seasickness first.

Even if I could get a cell signal, I don't have Bart's number to call for help.

So that leaves me to rely on Hudson, again. A man who may or may not want to kill me next. I think back to a few days ago when I sliced my arm open. He wanted to take the boat back to the mainland to get help. Or so he said.

Did he really mean to get me out on the boat so he could kill me and dump my body in the lake? Just like he did to Tess?

The difference is, he's not the beneficiary to a multi-million dollar insurance policy on my life, like he had with Tess. So he doesn't have a motive to kill me. I usually have good instincts about people, and nothing about Hudson has ever made me think he's capable of murder.

I pinch the bridge of my nose and close my eyes. It just doesn't make sense.

Regardless, Hudson is definitely not the person I thought he was. I mean, I was comfortable with him traveling all the time. I always imagined us in the trenches together, building a brighter future so we can have a big house and family like we always talked about.

Apparently that was all a lie. Now I have to wonder if he really has a job. What if he collected the money from the life insurance and has just been gallivanting around the country, hooking up with women in every city he visits?

The thought leaves a bitter taste in my mouth as I struggle to come to terms with the possibility that I've been deceived all this time. Given that I have nowhere else to go, I need to confront him about Tess. I want to hear his side of the story.

One thing that Tess made clear in her diary was that she was a little mentally unstable. And if she's admitting that even a little, it means she's probably downright crazy.

I take a calming breath. I need to know what Hudson has to say about all of this.

I pick up the diary and head to the bedroom. My phone is sitting on its charger on top of the nightstand. I pick it up and tuck it into my jeans. Just as I'm about ready open the door, the phone buzzes in my pocket.

I look at the caller ID. It's Claire. My heart skips a few more beats.

"Hello? Claire?"

"Natalie, I'm so glad I caught you. There's something you need to know."

"What is it?" I ask, my voice barely a whisper. My head

feels heavy, overwhelmed as I am with new information and uncertainty about the future.

"I followed up with the bank..." Her words hang in the air, each one like a weight pressing down on my chest. "Well, they're telling me they can't approve you because you've defaulted on your loan."

I stare at the plush grey carpet underneath my feet, its soft fibers seeming to mock me as confusion settles into my brain. I rack my memory, trying to recall any loans I may have taken out in the past.

"What loan?"

"I'm emailing you the paperwork now. Apparently, you cosigned for a loan with Declan alone for $500,000 to cover the properties you flipped together?"

Now my heart is really beating faster. *Loan?*

"Declan and I never took out a loan together," I say.

"Well, the bank has all the paperwork and it looks like you signed it. You can check the it yourself. It's been notarized."

The world begins to spin and blur around me as I struggle to stay vertical. My mind feels like it's being squeezed in a vice. I try to take a deep breath but my lungs feel constricted, as if someone is pressing down on my chest with all their weight. I'm having a full-blown heart attack or a panic attack. Either way, it doesn't matter because I can barely breathe, let alone speak.

"Natalie? Are you there?"

I take a shaky breath while she waits silently on the line.

"Claire, listen. Email me the paperwork. I'll call the bank as soon as I get back. I'm sure there's been some misunderstanding."

"Okay," says Claire. "I'm emailing you right now."

I hang up the phone and stare at myself in the mirror. I don't look good. My blonde hair hangs limply around my face, and I've lost some color. Instead of being bright blue, my eyes look somewhat cloudy.

I've got to pull myself together.

There has to be a way out of this. Not only did Declan take every last penny I own, but now it looks like I owe money to the bank. Money I can't afford to pay. Which means I will have to file for bankruptcy, or worse, I may go to jail. Suddenly, Hudson breaking up with me seems to be the least of my concerns.

My fists are clenched, knuckles turning white as I glare at the closed door in front of me. Fury boils within me. How could I have been so naive as to let Declan deceive me like this?

And now I realize that Hudson, or JJ, or whatever his name truly is, played me for a fool too. I can hear the old saying in my head: "Fool me once, shame on you; fool me twice, shame on me." Now I've been fooled twice.

I hear the door slam downstairs, which means Hudson is back. I grasp the diary and my phone close to my chest as I step into the hallway. It's time for the truth to come out.

23

"Nat," Hudson says as I reach the bottom of the stairs. His hair is matted down his face with water, and the rain is pouring off his jacket. He slips off his jacket and tosses it to the floor. "I've got some bad news," he says.

"Bad news? I have some bad news of my own," I say, my voice quivering with each word. He gives me a quizzical look and takes a few steps closer to me. We're now standing in the foyer. I take a few steps back.

"Natalie? Is everything okay?"

"Not exactly," I say, digging my heels into the worn wood floors.

"Listen, Natalie." He looks at me, a flash of fear crossing his eyes. "I think you were right about not being alone here. I saw someone, out on the island."

"Who?"

He shakes his head. "I don't know. They had a hat and trench coat on and it was hard to see." His face goes a shade paler. "I also thought I saw a gun."

I'm not sure what to say at this point, but something about my boyfriend, soon-to-be ex-boyfriend, looking fearful sends a chill down my spine.

"I've been telling you that since we got here!" I say, my voice belying my exasperation. "Who do you think it is? And what do they want with us?"

He shakes his head. "I don't know, but I have some ideas."

At this point, I'm not sure what to do. I need to confront him about what I found. Ask him about what happened to the missing girl that he was clearly married to. But at the same time, it's just us on this island. All we have is each other. I chew the inside of my cheek.

"There's something I've been wanting to tell you," he says.

I hold my breath. *Here goes.*

"I was married before..."

This is it, this is the moment he's going to tell me how he was married to Tess. Tess McDermott. And that he had something to do with her disappearance. Maybe even confess to her murder. Some of the anger I felt earlier dissipates. He's coming clean. *Finally.*

"It's actually a long story. Do you mind if we sit down?"

I nod silently. The less I say, the more he'll talk. That's probably the way I'm going to get to the bottom of this. Even though everything that comes out of his mouth is probably lies.

The two of us walk into the living room and settle on the couch. I've only been in this house for a couple of days, but this couch is something I'll probably remember forever given all the memories of diaries and cheating and conversations with my boyfriend, not to mention the giant gash that's probably going to leave a big crooked scar on my arm.

Hudson reaches over and grabs a glass of water that's sitting on the table. He takes a long drink. Again, I notice the spooked look in his eyes. His skin smells musty mixed with rain, and he has some mud smeared on his cheek. I resist the urge to reach up and touch his face.

Those days are over now.

Hudson breathes deeply. His chest rises and falls in a slow, deliberate motion. His face is calm and focused, his eyes on me.

"Like I said, I was married before. We actually knew each other from college. And then a few years ago, I ran into her again while I was entertaining some doctors in Chicago. We hit it off and began dating again. About six months later, she told me she was pregnant."

He closes his eyes for a moment and looks down at his hands. "Of course, I wanted to do the right thing, so I asked her to marry me. My parents weren't around anymore, neither was her father, and her mother was too ill to attend. So, the wedding came together pretty quickly."

He looks up at me, a tiny bit of guilt crossing his eyes. "We were married here, on the island."

I want to punch him in the face when he says it, but instead give him a terse nod.

"Keep going," I say.

"About a month after we were married, she lost the baby. We were both upset and disappointed, but she was devastated. She stayed in bed for weeks. I started to worry because she wasn't getting any better. So I called and talked to her doctor to see if he had some ideas for any ways that I could help her."

Hudson looks towards the window and then back at me. "He told me the truth. That she had never even been pregnant in the first place. She made the whole thing up."

I study his face carefully, looking for any signs that he might be lying.

"At first, I was really angry. I confronted her right away. She denied it, said the doctor was the one who was lying. But what bothered me the most was that she lied. I mean, I was in love with her. Maybe we would've gotten married right away but..."

Hudson shakes his head.

"Anyway, none of that matters now. She lied to me about being pregnant. And then she lied to me about other things too. You see, she came from a lot of money. Her family had a trust that had been passed down for generations. Old money. She spoiled me with fancy watches and even a new car. But as soon as I confronted her about the pregnancy, all that went away. She started to use her wealth like a weapon...and then she became extremely jealous. Like if I even smiled at the waitress when we were at a restaurant, she would scream at me and storm out of the room."

He swallows. "It was difficult to even be in the same room with her. I tried to be supportive. I found the best psychiatrist in the country to help her. But none of it worked. She seemed to only become more paranoid."

His voice changes, his shoulders slump. "A year ago I told her I wanted a divorce. But she threatened me. She told me that if I divorced her, she would ruin my life."

The sadness in his eyes runs deep. I'm so drawn into his story that I almost reach out and touch his hand. I forget for a moment what he did. Cheating on his wife... *with me.*

"So I started taking more business trips, trying to get

away from her craziness. She started making up these wild stories, like how I supposedly abused her, and then tried to use them to blackmail me."

I cross my arms as best I can, glaring at Hudson. If this story is supposed to make me feel better, it's not working so far. Hudson seems to notice my contempt.

"So, anyway, on one of those trips, that's when I met you." His voice softens. "And I was just so lonely, I couldn't help myself. I just...well, you know... Nat, I love you."

He looks deeply in my eyes and I'm drawn right back in. His words sound so genuine. So convincing. He straightens his back.

"I finally did it, though. I finally told her about eight months ago. I worked up the courage and told her that I wanted a divorce. I had my lawyer draw up all the paperwork. I thought she would freak out. Go crazy. Burn down our apartment."

His eyes get big and then narrow. "But she didn't. Something strange happened. She accepted it. Signed off on the divorce paperwork without a hearing in just a couple months. We had a prenup in place before we got married, so it was pretty simple."

So he's divorced...or so he says. I can always look up the filing to see if he's telling the truth. I take a deep breath, taking in everything that he's saying.

It's hard to believe it—that he's telling the truth. There are always two sides to every story, and at this point, I have no real reason to trust Hudson. But then again, I have no reason to trust this woman he married either.

"But I know how she works. Even though she signed the paperwork... I know she didn't let it go." He shakes his head, and his eyes turn dark. "I'm afraid she managed to trick me into bringing you here this week so she could get her revenge."

"But she's been missing for a year. I found her diary!"

He looks confused. "Missing? What do you mean? What diary?"

"Tess McDermott, your ex-wife. I found her diary in the master bedroom—"

Hudson is shaking his head profusely. "Tess? No, I was never married to Tess McDermott. She was my best friend from college. But we never—"

Now I'm the one who is confused.

"Then who were you married to?"

24

The storm roars outside, sending vibrations through the walls. Then, a sharp crack pierces through the chaos, followed by the sound of something heavy falling in the front yard. A shiver runs down my spine as I sit in the living room.

Hudson sits across from me, his gaze unmoving and his eyes wide with a mixture of confusion and disbelief. The dancing shadows from the fireplace play across his face, highlighting the slackness in his jaw. I can only imagine that my own expression mirrors his, my features frozen in a bewildered stare.

"I was married to Vivian Rockford," he says.

I'm literally stupefied at this point. I can't even begin to understand what he's saying.

"But the diary says..."

"What diary?"

"This one," I say, holding it up for him to see. He reaches out to touch it but I pull it away.

"I don't know where that diary came from, but it didn't

belong to Tess. And we were never married. We were friends. Good friends actually. I was devastated when she disappeared last year. I came out here looking for her."

"You had a close friend who disappeared a year ago and you didn't tell me about her? Why? Why did you lie every time I mentioned her name?"

Hudson shakes his head. "It's complicated. And I was going to tell you this week actually. I meant to tell you everything. About Vivian. And Tess. But then the storm, and you cut your arm... I didn't want to..."

Shakily, I rise to my feet, my limbs trembling with an overpowering mix of anger and confusion. My mind is already overloaded, unable to process any more information. I snatch the diary off the couch and thrust it into the air.

"This is Tess's diary. Your wife! And it says you killed her!"

Hudson shakes his head again, this time more insistently. "Nat, I'm telling you I was never married to Tess. I was married to Vivian. We all went to college together. But Vivian was my wife. She was an attorney from Chicago and six months ago we officially divorced, following a previous separation. And what I'm trying to tell you is—"

I place my hand on my hip and clench my jaw. He's obviously lying.

"If you were never married to Tess, then why are we here? I thought this was an Airbnb, for goodness' sake!"

A look passes across Hudson's face and then disappears quickly. He lowers his voice. "There's something else I need to tell you, and you're not going to like what you hear."

"Great," I say, my voice dripping with sarcasm. I brace myself.

"Please, sit down," he says quietly.

"Fine." I settle back onto the couch, although I keep myself on the edge of the seat. Hudson takes a deep breath.

"Tess and I have known each other since we were about fifteen. We met in boarding school. I didn't know her well then, but we ended up going to the same college. During that time, we hung out in the same circle of friends. After college, we stayed in touch. It was never romantic, or anything like that. She always had a boyfriend, and was briefly engaged. Anyway, when things went south with my marriage to Vivian, Tess reached out to check on me. I flew out here a few times to see her, just to have someone I could talk to about everything that was happening with Vivian. Then, about a year ago, she went missing."

Hudson reaches up and rubs his eyes with his right hand, straining with the last few words.

"I came out here to see if I could help. I even met with the police at one point." He looks down at his hands. "But they never found her."

Despite my anger, a part of me wants to reach over and grab his hands, console him. I remind myself that he was lying to me about Tess, which cools my sympathy. A few seconds of silence pass between us before he continues.

"Then, about a month ago, I received a notification letter from Tess's estate lawyer. The letter said Tess's body had been found and she had been officially proclaimed dead. It even included a copy of her death certificate. I was to come out here to her estate in Montana for a couple of days, in order to meet with the executor of her estate and sit for the reading of the will. He said I'd inherit a large sum of money. The lawyer also instructed me to bring a witness, even mentioned you by name." He rubs his hands up and down the top of his leg, then levels his eyes on mine. "I know it's weird, but I thought if I told you the whole truth about Tess and Vivian, you'd think I was crazy and run away. So I made up the part about the Airbnb—"

I let out a huff of air in disgust.

"I know it was stupid, Nat," he says, leaning towards me. I back up in my seat. "But I promise I was going to tell you everything. When we got to the island and the storm broke out, the lawyer sent me a message and said he wasn't coming. I wasn't sure what to do at that point. I kept looking for the right moment to tell you about why we're here, but then you cut your arm and..." He throws his hands up in the air, lets out an exasperated breath. "I just don't want to lose you, Nat. I love you."

I feel my resolve to hate Hudson and not believe anything he has to say waver ever so slightly. I tighten my arms, trying not to let myself get persuaded by his piercing blue eyes. It's a lot to take in. Two women from his past. A missing, presumed dead friend from college. A mentally unstable ex-wife. I shake my head, trying to think clearly through the noise.

"Really? You want me to believe that Tess McDermott left you some money? That's why we're here?"

"Yes," says Hudson. "I had to make my peace with her death. But the money... That could mean a new house for us. A future for us."

"A future? What, with me as your live-in girlfriend? You just told me yesterday you weren't ready to get married!"

"I know, but—"

"So you thought you'd bring me here to a romantic getaway at your dead friend's house?"

Hudson shakes his head. "I mean, when you put it like

that... But in the letter it said to bring you with me. That he wanted to meet with both of us."

"None of that makes sense, Hudson. I mean, I barely knew Tess existed until this week."

"I know, I know, the whole thing is strange. But I checked out the lawyer, and he was legit. Based out of Chicago, with one of those bigwig firms."

"But, isn't your ex-wife a lawyer too?"

"Yes..." I can see the realization fall across his face.

Ugh, men can be so blind sometimes.

"It has to be Vivian," he says, throwing up his hands. "She's messing with us."

At this point, I've reached my breaking point. I can't take any more lies. I don't know Tess and I don't know Vivian, and I don't want to. None of this has anything to do with me, except for the fact that Hudson has dragged me into it.

The storm is still raging outside, but at least I can get a head start on my packing. And then I'm going to do everything I can to get a cell signal and call Bart. I can't spend another second on this island.

"I don't want to hear any more about this," I say. "I don't believe you. And if you cheated on your ex-wife? What makes me believe that you're not going to cheat on me too?" I let out a disgusted sigh. "I'm going upstairs to pack. Don't follow me."

Hudson opens his mouth as if he's going to object to what I have to say. But he closes it again just as quickly. I turn from the couch and stomp towards the stairs. I look back for just a second, and he is just staring at me, his blue eyes blinking in the near darkness.

I make it to the top of the stairs before pausing to rest my hand on the carved wood banister. The stairs that Hudson so gently carried me up after my accident. All the times he eagerly came to my aid suddenly flood my brain.

I stand there for a moment, stuck between two options. Stay or go.

Be strong, Natalie. He doesn't deserve you.

But I can't deny it. I love him.

Maybe he's telling the truth and I should give him more time to explain, listen a little bit more to what he has to say. A small thudding sound comes from the living room.

"Hudson?" I call out from the staircase.

I pivot on my heel and carefully wind back down the stairs. I'll give him a little bit more time to explain things. Then I'll make my final decision.

I walk into the living room, expecting to see him waiting for me. But when I round the corner and the living room opens up in front of me, it's empty. *He was just here...*

"Hudson!"

I walk around the main floor, checking each room, even the bathroom. I can't imagine where he's disappeared to, but one thing is certain.

Hudson is gone.

PART II

VIVIAN

25

TWO YEARS EARLIER

"JJ, is that you?"

I am standing inside the dimly lit interior of the Sidebar, a trendy bar in downtown Chicago. My colleagues and I are gathered to celebrate our recent legal victory. It has been two years since I passed the bar exam, barely scraping by, but my family's influence has secured me a job at a prestigious law firm.

The pulsing beat of music and chatter fills the air, creating a lively atmosphere that seems to match the excitement of our group. Cheers and laughter ring out, and for a moment, all thoughts of work and responsibility fade away.

That's when I see him. Hudson Jared Jenkins. Or JJ, as we call him. *My college crush.*

Our eyes meet and he cuts through the crowded bar until he's standing just a few inches in front of me.

"Vivian? Wow, you look absolutely stunning," exclaims Hudson, his eyes roaming up and down my figure. I can't deny it—I feel confident and beautiful tonight. My tight-fitting cocktail dress hugs every curve while my best push-up bra accentuates my assets.

It is a stark contrast from my college days. Back then, I was struggling with depression issues and my unstable mother. I spent most of my nights buried in study hall, eating Chinese takeout and brownies for dinner. A diet that didn't do a lot for my figure. But after graduation I made a conscious effort to prioritize my mental and physical health by seeking therapy and hiring a personal trainer. And by the way men look at me now, I can tell it's paid off.

Hudson's timing couldn't have been more perfect.

"Thanks," I say, giving him my best smile.

"How have you been? It's been like, what, five years?" says Hudson. He is blushing slightly, which is a good sign.

It's impossible not to notice that Hudson still possesses the same rugged handsomeness from our college days. His dark hair is styled in a tousled manner, complementing his piercing blue eyes. He still has those broad shoulders that exude an air of confidence. When he smiles, I notice the dimple on his left cheek, a feature that always caught my attention in college.

Yes, I have noticed—perhaps become slightly obsessed with—Hudson in college, but he did not notice me. Hudson seemed to only have eyes for one woman—Tess McDermott, my sorority sister. The most beautiful and popular girl in our class.

In those days, Tess and I were close friends, but a small part of me couldn't help feeling envious of her. It wasn't just her family's wealth or her designer wardrobe that sparked this jealousy. No, it was something deeper— an intangible quality that seemed to radiate from her very being. Tess possessed a magnetic personality. She was the kind of person who could walk into a room and effortlessly command the attention of everyone around her. In contrast, I felt like nothing more than a wallflower, blending into the background while she shone like a star.

After college, we grew apart. I spent late nights studying in law school. Tess spent her time flitting around the world in her family jet. In fact, I haven't seen or talked to her in almost three years.

I always assumed she and Hudson got married, but as my eyes graze his left hand, I realize that Hudson is still single.

Looks like my night just got a little bit better.

"I've been great," I say. "We're actually out celebrating tonight. Would you like to join us?"

"Sure," he says, the lopsided smile falling across his face. He takes a swig of his drink. "What are we celebrating?"

"I just won my first case," I say. I give the bartender a nod and he immediately makes his way in our direction. It was one of the first things I noticed after I transformed my appearance from ugly duckling to swan...men seemed to suddenly be attentive to my every need.

"You won a case? As in you're a lawyer now?"

Hudson is impressed. I feel myself beaming with pride.

"Guilty as charged," I say, a wry smile crossing my face. Hudson laughs and orders himself another drink, and one for me too.

"I have to say, Vivian, I'm extremely impressed." By the way he can't take his eyes off me, I'm guessing it's not just because of my law degree.

"So," I purr, taking a slow sip of my martini and leaning in closer to him, "what have you been up to? Anything...exciting?"

We spend the rest of the evening locked in an intense conversation, our bodies pressed together in a dark corner of the bar. Our connection is instant and intense. Not only do we have a lot in common from our college days—mutual friends, professors—but we are both in the midst of building our careers. A shared bright future. I let him walk me home, but he leaves with nothing but my phone number.

The next day the guys from work give me a lot of flak about abandoning them that evening. But it was worth it. After that night, Hudson and I become inseparable.

Even though Hudson has to travel for work, we spend every night we can together, and when he is out of town, we FaceTime. In just a few weeks, we are caught up on the last five years apart. Of course, I leave out a few details, especially my time in Paris. But none of that matters.

All he needs to know is that I'm a successful lawyer now and have somehow managed to become the woman of his dreams.

26

ONE AND A HALF YEARS EARLIER

"Y ou'll need to write down your name, the date, the reason for your visit, and the resident you'll be visiting right here," says the woman behind the glass partition, pointing to a paper on a clipboard. Her tone is flat and not so friendly. She barely makes eye contact with me, and returns to her computer, fiercely typing away.

Then she looks up at me. "And I'll need to see your ID, please."

I dig into my wallet and hand her my driver's license. I take a look around the waiting room of the Connections Psychiatric Facility. The room is spacious, with high ceilings and large windows that offer a view of the surrounding lush green hills. The walls are adorned with tasteful paintings, adding an air of refinement to the space. The plush wood furnishings exude luxury and comfort.

The very best that money can buy.

I'm here today to visit my mother. She's been a resident here for the last five years. After a few what I would call 'episodes', it became clear that my mother would do better at a facility where she could receive care twenty-four seven. It wasn't something that was completely up to me. It was actually court ordered.

Now she spends her days here, pretty much drugged up beyond all recognition. But I know she's happier than dealing with the demons that haunted her before she came here.

When things in my life get really difficult, I find solace in visiting her. My mother, with her mind lost to dementia, is like a confessional—a place where I can spill my sins and secrets without fear of judgment. It's a twisted version of Catholic absolution, but it works for me. Her vacant gaze and blank expression make the perfect sounding board for my darkest thoughts.

Besides, I've been working with a psychiatrist myself, Dr. Sloan. She tells me that talking about how you feel to someone or keeping a diary can really help. I don't completely trust her yet to tell her everything, and I refuse to keep a diary, but visiting my semi-comatose mother and confessing my bad choices is the next best thing.

"Mrs. Rockford, you can go in now," says the woman as she scrapes open the glass partition and hands me my ID.

A neatly dressed orderly in all white appears at my side and leads me down the hallway to my mother's room. This is more of a high-profile institution, and so even though the patients are basically prisoners, you would never know. The carefully designed space is actually quite welcoming.

I open the door to my mother's suite and see her sitting by the window, a shell of her former self. Her once vibrant blonde hair is now a dull shade of gray, slicked back tightly into a bun. The same pearl earrings dangle from her ears, a symbol of past elegance now tarnished. She is draped in a matching sweater set, buttoned up to the neck.

But when she turns to me, I see a flicker of recognition in her weary eyes, and for a moment I am grateful that at least here, they are taking care of her. For someone who is on a massive amount of drugs, she still looks pretty. But that's my mother. She's always been beautiful.

"Hello, Mother," I say. "I brought you something."

I set her favorite raspberry-filled chocolates on the table next to her favorite chair. Taking a seat in a tiny chair across from her, I gaze out the large window in front of us.

She doesn't immediately meet my gaze, but I have grown accustomed to that. During my last visit, the doctors informed me that the dementia has worsened. They have prescribed a medication to help her feel more at ease, but it also seems to make her a bit numb. After some time, she gradually turns her head towards me.

"Hello," she says in a monotone voice. I scoot my chair a little bit closer to her.

"Mother, I have so much to tell you," I say, leaning towards her. "Remember how I told you I got married six months ago?" I know she doesn't remember, but I continue on. "His name is Hudson Jared Jenkins. So I guess now you could say that I am Mrs. Jenkins. But not really, of course. I kept our last name. You always told me to never give up the Rockford family name."

If my mother was mentally here, I'm sure this would have pleased her. My hands get a little clammy, even though I know she can't really hear me. I still am nervous about what I have to say.

"Things haven't exactly gone as planned. You see, Hudson and I had been dating for six months before he proposed. And I knew he was the one...I just knew it. So I was hoping to speed our engagement along. I wanted to give Hudson a reason to propose sooner rather than later. I mean, we we're both in our thirties and all of our friends are getting married and having kids..."

My mother blinks slowly, which I take as an acknowledgment that she hears me.

"Anyway, I woke up one morning and realized I was late on my period. I had been off birth control for a month, so I thought maybe... Maybe I was pregnant."

I slide the palms of my hands, which start to sweat, along my pants. "So I took a pregnancy test. It was negative. And about a week later, my period did come. But the whole experience gave me an idea. What if I did get pregnant? Hudson's an old-fashioned kind of guy and I know he'd do the right thing."

I lean closer to my mother. "Besides, isn't that how you and Dad got married? You found out you were pregnant with me?"

For a moment, I think I see a flicker of emotion pass across my mother's delicate features. But then her face smooths out again, the blank expression returning.

And here comes the confessing my sins part...

"Anyway, I went online and ordered one of those fake positive pregnancy tests. I know it sounds...unconventional, but I just figured we could be married and pregnant in a few months anyway. So what's the harm in speeding things along?"

I blow some air out through my lips. "I showed the positive test to Hudson and told him I was pregnant. He was shocked, of course, but happy for us. And just as I had suspected, he did the right thing and proposed to me the very next week."

Mother blinks at me with her empty blue eyes.

"Hudson and I had already talked about starting a family together. I just assumed a few weeks later we would get pregnant again." I slump in my chair. "But as it turns out, we didn't get pregnant. And a month after the honeymoon I had to tell him something, because he was asking about doctor's appointments and why I didn't have any morning sickness."

I lick my lips, which have suddenly become dry.

"So I told him that I had a miscarriage and that my doctor had confirmed we lost the baby. He was so supportive and caring—another reason to love him. I told him we could keep trying. But after months of trying with no luck, I became depressed. Hudson tried to cheer me up. He even bought me a little kitten. I named her Gucci, you know, after your favorite brand."

I watch for some recognition in her eyes, but she continues to watch me with an empty stare. My mother used to keep an entire closet full of designer brands. Most of it, I sold to a consignment store when she moved in here.

"Anyway, we stopped having sex, which didn't help my case either. Hudson was worried about me, so one day he called my doctor."

My cheeks burn a bit as I continue. This part still makes me angry. *People can be so stupid.*

"And guess what happened? Because he was my husband, that idiot doctor told him that I was never pregnant. Hudson was furious. He said I lied to him, trapped him into this marriage."

Tears begin to sting my eyes. That part still hurts. I lean forward and grab my mother's hands.

"Mom, he said I was *mentally unstable*. You of all people should know that's not true."

I lean back again. "And I know it's not true. I'm not unstable. I hate that he says that, and even worse, the idea that he's telling his friends makes my blood boil. And so one night, after he told me I'm crazy for the hundredth time, I snapped. I slapped him as hard as I could across the face. He said some pretty awful things to me then and even pushed me. He *pushed* me!"

I ball my hands into tight fists and slam them onto my thighs. "I didn't spend years studying law just to become a victim of some wife abuser," I say, shaking my head in disbelief. My mother's expression remains blank, and I can't tell if she's understanding any of this. But at least it feels good to speak the truth.

"Now he's telling me he wants a divorce. I can't let him do that to me. I'll be humiliated. He'll run around and tell everyone I'm crazy. It will ruin my reputation."

With a bit of effort, I squeeze out a few tears that slide down my cheeks. The silly little girl in me wants my mother to see my pain, to come back and comfort me. Her big blue eyes blink slowly, devoid of any emotion as she utters her words with a cold detachment that shatters my heart.

"I'm sorry," she says. I swallow the lump in my throat.

"I'm sorry too, Mother," I say. I straighten up, and tuck a strand of hair behind my ear. "Anyway, I'm meeting with my friend John tomorrow and we're going to come up with a plan to fix this mess."

I clasp her hands. "And don't worry about me, okay? I'll get this figured out."

I rise from my chair and lean in to give my mother a peck on the cheek. As I head towards the door, an orderly arrives with a tray of food for her lunch. My gaze falls upon the meal, a spread of braised fish, mashed sweet potatoes, and asparagus. Given my mother's frail appearance, I have doubts about whether she'll actually eat any of it. I also notice a small rose in a vase on the tray, which shows that they are—at the very least—trying to make her feel better.

My heels echo down the hallway as I trek back to the lobby.

Dr. Sloan is right. I do feel slightly better. It felt really good to tell the whole truth and get it off my chest. But as I pass by a line of rooms with patients gazing vacantly out their windows, I make a firm decision: I will not end up in a place like this.

The end of my story is not going to be the same as my mother's. Because despite everything that Hudson has said, I'm not crazy. And I'm going to do everything in my power to make sure everyone knows it.

27

"I 'll have another, please," I say to the cocktail waitress, who politely nods and heads back to the bar. My best friend John and I huddle in the corner of a trendy steakhouse in Chicago, the dim lighting casting shadows on our faces. I asked John to meet me after the encounter with my mother yesterday. I need someone in my corner, and he has always served as my unwavering ally. Especially after what happened in Paris a few years ago—he owes me for that.

"Are you sure you want to order another one of those martinis?" John says. I glance down at the empty glass in front of me, feeling the warm buzz of alcohol coursing through my veins. I supposed he's right. I am on my third martini and he's still nursing his first.

"Desperate times call for desperate measures."

John smiles at me and cues the waitress to bring another for him as well. That's what I love about John—he gets me. We've been pretty tight friends since law school. John comes from a similar background to mine. Family pedigree, old money, trust fund.

But neither of us wanted to sit around drinking bloody marys by the country club pool. No, we're both smarter than that. So the two of us ended up in law school and immediately bonded over our life experiences and, of course, our eccentric tastes.

Especially John's eccentric taste.

"So let me get this straight. He wants to get a divorce. Isn't that what you want too?"

"Yeah, I suppose so," I say while touching my forehead. "Well, it's complicated. I still have feelings for him..."

It's true, I do still love Hudson. When things were good between us, they were great. We had a lot of fun together, especially in bed. But I don't mention any of this to John.

He has always been attracted to me, especially after I transformed during law school. And to be fair, John wouldn't be the worst-looking guy I've dated. He always looks sharp in his three-piece suit and tortoiseshell glasses, and he's kind of cute in a nerdy way.

But for me, the spark just isn't there. I've only ever wanted a friendship with John, and he is a wonderful friend. Especially for someone like me, who has trouble making friends anyway.

"But besides my broken heart," I say with a dramatic wave of my hand, "the thing that bothers me the most is that Hudson is telling everybody that I'm mentally unstable. That I should be in the same psychiatric hospital as my mother. He wants to file for divorce on account of insanity. Can you believe that?"

John gives me a smirk. Even if he agrees, he'll never say so.

"Okay, so what is it that you want, then?"

"First? I want to control the story. You know what it's like in our circle. Everyone's probably talking about us already, but they're only hearing his side of the story—that I'm some lunatic who tricked him into marriage. And it won't be hard for them to believe I'm mentally unstable—as he says—given my mother's situation. I've done my best to keep that under wraps, but it won't take long for everyone we know to put two and two together."

The thought alone was enough to turn my stomach into knots. We get together once or twice a year with all of our friends from college. People I met there and friends I've known since prep school. Last year the big scandal was around Pepper Sorensen, whose family filed for bankruptcy. She couldn't even afford to make it to our weekend getaway in Bali to defend herself. Or maybe she was too embarrassed to come. Either way, I saw a group of people who had been her closest friends in college turn on her in a heartbeat. If they hear what Hudson has to say about me? My cheeks burn with embarrassment at just the thought of such a scenario playing out.

"I want the story behind our divorce to be about him doing something awful, not me."

"Why do you care, Viv?"

I glance away, feeling a twinge of guilt at his words. Perhaps it's because I've put in so much effort to transform into the person I am now: meticulously crafting my appearance, earning my law degree. I've surpassed my own expectations and risen above being labeled as a privileged rich kid whose mother is in a mental institution. But if Hudson spreads a bunch of rumors about me? All that will be ruined.

Either way, I'm not sure John would understand. I don't

think anyone has ever questioned his intelligence or his sanity. I refocus my attention on him.

"I don't know why. But it just bugs me to no end. All of them laughing behind my back. Hudson whispering how he divorced that crazy Vivian Rockford. It would be humiliating."

"Come on, Viv, you're smarter than that. They'll talk about you no matter what."

He has a point.

"You're smart too, John," I say, dipping my chin in his direction. "But it doesn't mean we always make good choices."

John leans back in his seat, adjusting his tortoiseshell glasses. He's smart, there's no doubt about it. In fact, he graduated top of our class in law school. But he's more than that. John is shrewd. He can look at a situation and see all the possible outcomes like in a game of chess.

He ended up taking a job with his family's firm in Chicago, nearby to where I worked.

We used to get together regularly for dinner and drinks. But everything changed when I met Hudson and got married. Suddenly, my former friend John was no longer a regular in my life.

It wasn't until my problems with Hudson reached a breaking point that I reached out to him for help, hoping he would still be there for me. He immediately made himself available.

"Okay, what's the second reason?"

"I want him to pay for how he's treated me. He doesn't deserve to walk away from this without punishment."

It isn't fair for Hudson to label me as mentally unstable to our entire circle of friends and then dump me on the side of the road like trash. It might take some convincing, but I believe I could convince John that helping me destroy Hudson is an act of justice.

John is rubbing his chin. I can see the gears turning in his brain.

"The prenup is pretty solid, right?"

I nod.

"What about a life insurance policy?"

Our fresh set of drinks arrive, and I immediately take another sip. The alcohol slides down my throat, causing a slight tingling sensation. I suddenly become aware of how hungry I am. My stomach feels empty.

"I set up a policy for him after we married."

"Death benefit?"

"Two million."

John lets out a long whistle. "You're a generous lady."

I roll my eyes. "Let's order food."

We order a plethora of appetizers. Oysters on the half shell, shrimp cocktail and a few wagyu beef tacos the waitress said are "to die for." Between my mother's deteriorating condition and the stress of the divorce, I suddenly feel a primal desire for food.

After the waitress leaves, John returns his gaze to me.

"Okay, we can work with that," he says, taking a swig from his glass. "Let's say Hudson has been eyeing that life insurance money for some time now. You said he pushed you...which shows he can be violent. Is premeditated murder such a stretch?"

I have to admit, I'm intrigued by the idea. The thought of Hudson going to jail for something like premeditated murder feels pretty satisfying. Not to mention the fact that

I'd have a pretty juicy story to explain our divorce. *It's tempting.*

"I see where you're going with this," I mull it over while taking a sip of my fresh drink. "But Hudson makes pretty good money at his job. And I'm not sure if anyone would believe he's capable of murder. Plus, if we got caught, I'd be in serious trouble."

John nods slowly. "Okay, that's fair. Let's go for something a little less macabre." He bites his lip in contemplation, his gaze scanning the room.

"How about this? You catch Hudson cheating on you. We get proof. It's certainly a reason for divorce." His eyes twinkle.

The thought of Hudson cheating on me feels like a punch to the gut. The idea throws me off balance for a moment and I nearly spill my drink. I think I might have over-served myself. That food had better come quickly. John continues on.

"Besides, isn't there an infidelity clause in your prenup?"

I nod, the notion snapping me back to reality. I feel a bit of excitement bubble up in my chest. The *infidelity clause.* Yes, it was one of the lifestyle clauses my lawyer added to the prenup. If states that if Hudson cheats, he has to pay a penalty. Fifty thousand dollars, to be exact. I'm sure that would make him think twice about how he treated me.

"John, you're a genius." I lean in slightly and gently brush John's hands with my own. A small smile tugs at the corners of his lips. "I'll keep my reputation and destroy his. And he'll literally pay for how he's treated me."

A few steaming plates of food arrive. Just in time too. I'm feeling a little lightheaded from all the martinis and I need some food to soak up the alcohol. I need my wits about me right now.

"So," I say, tucking a napkin onto my lap, "how do we do it?"

"Didn't you say Hudson used to have one of those dating apps on his phone?"

A smile tugs at the corner of my mouth as I listen to John lay out the steps in our plan. I will need to get access to Hudson's phone, so I can re-activate his *SwipeYes* dating app account. Hudson is a bit disorganized when it comes to his phone. He never deletes *anything*. This used to drive me mad. Now? I'm glad he didn't listen to me when I nagged him to clean it up.

Once that's done, John has a friend who can hack into his account and make connections on Hudson's behalf. All of this activity would be completely untraceable. Not to mention, there's no way anyone could link it back to me. Given my plan to enact the infidelity clause from our prenup, that's important.

I know Hudson has a lot of clients in Atlanta, so I think that would be the perfect place for him to meet someone. I have to admit, the whole plan is a bit difficult for me to handle. The thought of pushing my husband into the arms of another woman isn't easy to stomach. Even though I'm going to pay for it tomorrow, I order another martini.

A fleeting thought crosses my mind, tempting me to invite John back to my place for a more intimate setting. But I quickly push it aside—John is not my type. He's much better as a friend. Regardless, he's going to take care of all the details and set everything in motion.

All I have to do now is sit back and watch our plan unfold.

28

ONE YEAR AGO

The loud banging on the door won't stop. I pull my pillow over my head, but I can't drown out the sound. I climb out of bed and wrap a bathrobe around myself. I glance over my shoulder, my eyes grazing over the naked body of the man still in my bed. I push my hair out of my face and make my way to the front door.

"I'm coming. Keep your pants on," I grumble. Before I pull the door open, I wipe the drool off my mouth. I'm sure I look like hell right now. The banging returns again, and I finally rip open the door.

John stands before me, dressed in his signature three-piece suit and brown-rimmed glasses. He must have just left the office to come here.

"Wow, Vivian, you look terrible," he remarks.

I can't help but bite my lip. I know he's speaking the truth, but it still stings.

"It's nice to see you too, John," I say. "Come on inside."

I move out of the way and let John enter the room. He's sporting a new cologne that smells much better than my stale, alcohol-laced morning breath. Gucci suddenly appears, purring as she weaves her way through his legs. He reaches down to pat her.

As we make our way from the hallway into the living room, the man I spent the night with emerges from the bedroom. *Derick? Dustin?* Honestly, I can't remember, which isn't a good sign. I rake my eyes over his muscular arms and wavy brown hair. He's not exactly marriage material, but man, he is sexy.

"Hey, I've got to get to work." he says, his voice low and raspy. He walks over and gives me a kiss on the cheek. "I'll call you."

"Right, see you later," I say as I close the door behind him.

I turn and face John. He looks at me squarely, his eyes sweeping across my unkempt hair, streaked mascara, and loosely wrapped bath robe.

"You're sleeping with a bartender from the Sidebar now?"

I feel myself blush ever so slightly. I shrug. "What can I say? Desperate times call for—"

"Desperate measures. I know, Vivian," John says, rolling his eyes. "Listen, I'm going to order us a deep-dish pizza. You go take a shower, and then we need to talk."

I plaster a fake smile on my face and quickly escape to the shower. John is always there for me, which I appreciate. But he can also be a little judgmental, which I *don't* appreciate.

The scalding water burns away the remnants of last night's alcohol haze, but it can't erase the choices I made. As I take some aspirin and chase it down with water, I try to ignore the sinking feeling in my stomach. Hopefully a greasy slice of deep-dish pizza will help.

I walk into the kitchen where John is leaning over his phone. He pushes a large Gatorade across the table towards me.

"Thank you," I say.

"Aren't you supposed to be at work today?" he asks.

I settle into one of the barstools at the large marble island.

"I'm taking a leave of absence, a sabbatical if you will," I say.

John looks at me, his eyes wide. "But you love your job."

I shrug. "Sometimes."

"Viv, you have got to pull yourself together. This is ridiculous."

"I know, I know." I hold up my hand. "I just need some time."

I chug my drink and set it on the island with a dramatic sigh. John looks at me.

"You know he did it, right?" I say. "He took the bait. He's sleeping with her."

Everything that John and I had planned went flawlessly. Getting into Hudson's phone was the tricky part. Given his travel schedule and the tension at home, I have barely seen my husband, much less have access to his phone. But while he was showering one day, I was able to get into his phone and re-activate his *SwipeYes* account. After that John's friend with the hacking skills took over and began to link up Hudson with a few profiles John and I had selected.

Before I could second-guess our decision to set him up, Hudson was having coffee with some blonde-haired real estate bimbo from Atlanta. We used a private investigator friend of John's named Sam to follow him. It only took a week to get the evidence we needed that he was cheating.

It all went according to our plan, which was fine in theory. But when Sam brought me the photos of the two of them together a few days ago? I sort of lost it. I got way too drunk and, before I could embarrass myself, took a leave of absence from work.

"This is exactly what you wanted, Vivian," John says, looking at me incredulously. "He's sleeping with this girl, now we have the proof, and you can get a divorce, walk away, and start over. Reputation intact."

I can hear the words coming out of his mouth, and they all sound perfect in theory. But, when I saw those pictures, something inside me shattered. I couldn't fathom that Hudson would actually go through with it; that he would actually betray me.

Even after John and I had agreed to go through with our plan, I couldn't shake the desperate longing to reconnect with Hudson. My heart ached for the way he used to look at me, full of adoration instead of disdain. I was still angry about the way he treated me after the 'miscarriage', but all the things I loved about him were still there too.

There were nights when I would find myself on the floor of our bedroom, an empty bottle of wine and Gucci next to me, flipping through the photos from our wedding album. How could something so beautiful become so ugly?

"I still love him," I say. As soon as the words come out of my mouth, I realize how pathetic they sound. John gives me a sympathetic look.

"I know," he says, his face softening. "But at some point, you're going to have to leave it behind you and move on.

Quitting your job and sleeping with the neighborhood bartender isn't the right way to do it."

I know he's right, but I just can't quite muster up the strength to do the right thing, not yet.

The doorbell rings, and our lunch has arrived. I eagerly take the box of pizza from the delivery guy and carry it to the kitchen island. The two of us sit side by side, pulling our first slices straight out of the box.

"Mmm, this takes me back to our days studying for the bar," I say with a nostalgic smile.

John chuckles, his warm brown eyes lighting up. "You always did have a weakness for deep-dish pizza."

We eat a few more slices in contented silence, the tangy sauce and gooey cheese slightly reviving my spirits.

"Well, I do have some news," I eventually say, wiping my mouth with a napkin. "I'm going on a little trip this weekend."

John arches one of his dark eyebrows at me. "Oh really? Where are you off to?"

"Well," I say, pausing to swallow a mouthful of cheese. "You're not going to believe this, but I was invited to a girls' weekend in Montana."

John drops his slice of pizza back in the box with a thud.

"Oh Vivian, you're not talking about Tess McDermott's place, are you?"

"Yes, John. I am talking about Tess McDermott's private island in Montana." I give him a hard look. "She invited me out for a girls' weekend, and I think I need to go."

"You really think that's a good idea? That's where you and Hudson were married, for goodness' sake. In your current state..."

"I can handle myself, I promise. This is exactly what I

wanted. I will tell Tess everything, show her the photos, and she'll know what a jerk Hudson really is."

John leans back in his seat and lets out an exasperated sigh. "Fine, but promise me if things get weird, you'll call me, okay?"

"I promise, John." I lean over and give him a little peck on the cheek. "And thanks for the pizza."

"Anytime," he says, a slight blush in his cheeks. He stands up from his seat. "Listen, I have to get back to work. You take care of yourself, okay?"

"I will," I say. I walk him to the door and shut it quietly when he leaves.

What I don't tell John is that Tess didn't exactly invite me to the estate. We've been texting back and forth and she mentioned she was staying out in Montana. Hudson's out of town this weekend. So, I thought I would surprise her and come out for a little girls' weekend.

I want her to hear my side of the story. Then she can spread the truth to everyone we know. The truth that Hudson is a cheating scoundrel and he ruined our marriage —not me.

29

SIX MONTHS AGO

The black umbrella trembles in my grip as the rain pounds down from the sky, a relentless torrent that seems to mirror the ache in my heart. Why does it always seem to rain when there's a funeral? A more sensitive soul might suggest it's the tears of God, sharing in our grief.

Me? I chalk it up to bad luck. Something that I seem to have in spades lately.

I watch with numb disbelief as they lower my mother's body into the ground, her final resting place inside a shiny mahogany casket. The funeral is painfully small, a stark reminder of how few people were left in my mother's life. I stand among mostly strangers, struggling to hold back tears as the loss of her sinks in.

The official cause of her death is a heart attack, but it feels more like a cruel twist of fate. Her heart, always fragile, was further weakened by the medication she was prescribed. It turns out the cure for her suffering mind also led to her death.

The thought of legal action crosses my mind, but what's the point? In reality she was already gone, trapped in a haze of sedatives. Was there even a part of her left to fight for? My anger and grief merge into an overwhelming sense of helplessness.

John stands solemnly beside me, the only friend who bothered to come and support me at my mother's funeral. We watch in silence as the shovels scrape the last remnants of dirt onto her casket. The funeral director nods at me, signaling that it's time to leave. I release the white rose I've been clutching and watch it fall into the grave with a sickening thud.

It hasn't been the best day. Not only did I have to bury my mother, but I also received confirmation from my divorce attorney that all the legal proceedings were finalized.

My marriage is officially over. I stare through the rain at the giant hole in the ground before me. *Life really has a way of kicking you while you're down.*

"Come on," John says, placing a hand on my back. "Let's go have a drink."

The two of us make our way down the sidewalk to where a long black limousine is waiting. John holds the umbrella over my head as I climb in the back.

"Four Seasons Chicago, please," I say to the driver.

John is sitting next to me brushing the rain off his shoulders. "The Four Seasons, huh? What happened to your apartment?"

"I sold it," I say.

John hesitates, as if he wants to say something, but ultimately decides against it. Maybe it's for the best; I'm not sure I can handle any questions about my life choices. I just need to focus on burying my mother. Besides, he doesn't have much room to judge me at the moment anyway.

The drive from the cemetery to the hotel takes around thirty minutes, during which neither of us speaks. But his presence is comforting to me. I stare out of the window, watching as the relentless rain drenches the city in a dreary gray hue. Even Chicago loses its sparkle when it rains. As we arrive at the hotel, the doorman opens the car door and I step out, taking hold of John's arm as we stroll inside.

"To the bar?"

I try to muster up a smile but I can't quite bring one to my lips. "You read my mind."

We sidle through the double doors, which close behind us with a hushed thud, muffling the street noise from outside. I immediately scan the room to see if I recognize anyone I know. Thankfully, the bar is pretty much empty, save for a handful of businessmen at the other end of the room.

I eye the polished mahogany bar lined with red velvet stools that stretches the length of the room. John trails behind me as I sink into the plush cushion of my seat and place our usual order; vodka martini, extra dirty, for me and a Negroni for John.

The dimly lit bar provides a sense of security, shielding us from the outside world for just a little while longer. The sound of ice clinking in glasses and low murmurs of conversation nearby create a soothing background soundtrack.

I slowly sip my martini, savoring the silence. John, on the other hand, seems to be itching to talk. I slowly look up from my drink, making eye contact with him.

"So, are you going to tell me why you sold your place?"

I set my glass down, letting out a heavy sigh. "Too many

memories," I say, fiddling with the edge of my napkin. "I'm ready for a change."

John raises his eyebrows at me. "What kind of change?"

"I'm thinking of moving somewhere warmer...maybe somewhere south."

John's expression gives away the fact that he is well aware of what I am contemplating. I admire his composure as he remains silent, patiently waiting for me to reveal my plans to him.

"Okay," he says, taking a sip of his own drink. "How far south are we talking? Miami? Costa Rica?"

"Too hot," I declare, flicking a bit of lint off my sleeve.

To be honest, I can't escape the constant thoughts of Hudson, the affair that tore apart my marriage. Now, with my mother gone, the weight of unresolved issues is crushing me. Is it my lawyer's instinct or just sheer stubbornness that won't let me move on? Regardless, I refuse to let Hudson and his new bimbo girlfriend ride off into the sunset while I suffer in silence. No, I'll fight tooth and nail to make sure they never find happiness again.

"I have something different planned, John," I say. He takes a deep breath, clearly bracing himself for what I have to say. I smile, reveling in his discomfort. "You might need to order another drink."

"Fine." John rolls his eyes and nods to the bartender. The piano player starts playing a familiar Sinatra tune. I turn my head to listen, the lyrics playing in my mind "...You're flying high in April, shot down in May..."

That sounds about right.

Hudson loved that song. Of course it would be playing now, twisting the knife that's already in my heart. We listen in silence for a few minutes while the bartender makes us another round. When he places the drinks in front of us, John gives me an impatient look.

"Okay, let's have it," he says.

"The thing is... Hudson doesn't deserve to be happy. He took everything from me. I'll never be a new bride again. I may never be married again or have children or a big house or..." I look down at the drink in front of me. "I may never fall in love again."

John reaches over and touches my hand. "Of course you will."

I shake away the sorrow that's threatening to snuff out my anger. "And that slut that he's been hooking up with—"

John cocks his head to the side, giving me a knowing look. "Oh, the one you set him up with on the online dating site?"

"Doesn't matter how it happened, John." I roll my eyes, brushing him off. "The fact that he jumped in bed with her so quickly... She doesn't deserve to be happy either. I want to make both of them pay. But I can't execute this plan by myself. I need a partner."

I give him the highlights of my plan in just a few minutes. John listens intently, a look of dread crossing his eyes. When I'm finished, I wait patiently for him to respond. The look he's giving me isn't a good sign.

"Vivian, listen to me, you have got to let this go. It's not a good idea. Messing with other people's lives–"

"Messing with other people's lives? They messed with mine first. They deserve everything that's coming to them."

"Bankruptcy? Jail?" His eyes go wide. He leans back in his seat. "I'm not saying they don't deserve it. But do you really think you can get away with this and not get yourself in trouble?"

"Of course I do," I say, flicking a lock of hair over my shoulder. I place a hand on his leg. "What's the point of going to law school, if not learning how to bend the rules a bit?"

John shakes his head. I already know what he's going to say.

"No way, Vivian. I'm telling you this as a friend. You cannot do this. It sounds...well, you know how it sounds. I'm not going to say the word but—"

"John, you have to help me. I am asking you for this one last favor."

He shakes his head again. "It's not a good idea. I can't do it, Viv. I can't be a part of this. I care about you too much for that."

He signals the bartender, who approaches our table. He requests the bill and retrieves his credit card to settle the tab. I sit back and let him handle the transaction, but there's no chance of me allowing him to leave just yet.

"John, you have to help me." I place my hand on his arm. "You owe me, remember? Remember what happened in Paris?"

John's head snaps towards me. His eyes flash with intensity. "We swore we would never talk about that."

"I'm not talking about it," I say, sitting up a little bit straighter in my stool. "I am just saying that you owe me for what I did to get you out of that mess."

He shakes his head in a slow back-and-forth motion, the weight of his expensive black suit pulling at his shoulders. I can tell he's finally starting to crumble under my pressure. After all these years, I know John well enough to read his body language like a book. He takes a deep breath and loosens his tie, a sure sign of surrender.

"Vivian... My dear Vivian. The things I do for you."

"So you'll do it?"

John releases a drawn-out sigh. He fiddles with the frames of his glasses, adjusting them on the bridge of his nose. "Why don't we order some dinner and we'll talk about it."

Technically he didn't say yes in that moment, but I knew I had him. Like I said, John's always had a thing for me. Plus, he owes me a favor. A favor I have been saving for a time like this.

We seek refuge at a secluded table in the darkest corner of the bar. The hours slip by as we devour our dinner, plotting and scheming. By the time our plates are cleared, our plan is woven together into a perfect little tapestry of deceit.

"Six months?" he finally says, a slight twinkle in his eyes. He won't admit it, but John loves a good revenge plan. He's going to enjoy this too.

"Six months...and then I promise I'll let it go."

John smirks at me. I can tell by the flush in his cheeks he's a little drunk. I don't think he's convinced I'll let it go, but he's with me regardless. He raises his wine glass.

"To you, Vivian Claire Rockford, the most formidable woman I know."

I smile and raise my glass, tapping his. "And you too, John Declan Roberts, the best friend a girl could ask for."

30

THREE WEEKS EARLIER

I look up from my desk as Natalie barges into the CenterPoint Atlanta real estate office, her entrance snapping my head to attention. I've been struggling to stay awake at my desk recently; the job has become so monotonous. It's been a few months since I started working here—pushing around paperwork, making phone calls, fetching coffee.

This part of the plan fell into place rather neatly. At first I thought maybe I'd get a real estate license and a job at her office. It was crucial for me to be involved in some capacity for our plan to succeed. I would have had to pull a few strings to get a good fake license, but we could have made it work. When I saw Natalie posted a job for an assistant...well, it was almost too easy.

No one, including Natalie, knows my true identity. They are unaware that I am a lawyer or that I was once married to Natalie's current boyfriend. It surprises me how well I have been able to keep everything under wraps.

Today she seems unusually happy. She left a couple

hours ago, off to have lunch with Hudson. I can't stop myself from rolling my eyes at her bright eyes and flush cheeks. *She's in love.* Every time she goes off to have lunch with him, it feels like a knife twisting in my gut.

But mostly it's been fun. I've never been in a situation before where I could completely be somebody else. I let my hair color go natural and stopped doing my nails. I even downgraded my wardrobe. Let's face it, no one would buy my charade if I showed up in an Armani suit.

Honestly, my performance as Claire, the ever-eager-to-please office assistant could rival that of any actress I've seen on screen.

I'll take my Oscar with a side of revenge, thank you very much.

John, on the other hand, has been miserable. For whatever reason, he feels some sort of guilt for tricking 'poor Natalie' into losing all her money. I've really had to step up my game to keep him happy. I've been having him over to my little apartment on the weekends, when we get drunk together and binge watch Netflix. And a little flirtation goes a long way with him.

Natalie approaches my desk. I straighten my shoulders and adjust my glasses. Time for another acting performance.

"How was lunch?" I ask, giving her my brightest smile.

"Great," she says, brushing a bit of bleached blonde hair off her shoulder. She's glowing with some news, I can tell. Either that, or the two of them had sex over her lunch hour.

Disgusting.

"Guess what?" she says, dropping her handbag on my desk.

"Hmm?"

"Hudson is going to take me away for a few days. A romantic getaway, he called it."

So he took the bait. My heartbeat flutters. This is what I've been waiting for.

"Oh really," I say, leaning forward and tucking my hand under my chin. "Where is he taking you?"

"Oh, it's this fabulous Airbnb in Montana. He sent me some photos last week. It's beautiful. Looks like a French-style chateau set on a private island..."

She drones on about the place. I feel a rush of pleasure. *It totally worked.* This part of the plan was tricky, getting Hudson out to the McDermott estate. But there wasn't anywhere else in the world that I could imagine dealing Hudson the final blow.

John and I put together a certified letter under the name of one of our attorney friends. The letter stated he was to inherit a hefty sum from Tess's estate, who sadly had been found dead. All he had to do was show up the second week in October, and bring someone with him as a witness. Of course, all of the estate amenities would be at his disposal, per Tess's request.

It was a fun bit of fiction to write. But of course, I was holding my breath, waiting to see if it would work. Hudson, who is always looking for a chance at some extra cash, seems to have gone for it, hook, line and sinker.

"That sounds fantastic," I say. "Maybe he'll even propose."

Natalie tips her shoulders and smiles, saying nothing. But it's clear by the look on her face that she's thought about it. Even better. *The higher the stakes the harder the fall.*

"Anyway, I'll be out of town the week of October fourteenth," she says, pointing to the calendar on my desk. "Can you put that in the calendar for me?"

"Of course," I say, pulling out my pen. "I'll do it right away."

"Thanks, Claire," she says. "You're the best."

I summon up a believable smile. Sometimes this acting thing is a little bit harder than I let on. Especially on days like today where I'm basically helping to plan a romantic getaway for my ex-husband and his new girlfriend. But I know it's all going to pay off in the end.

"Hey, do you have any plans tomorrow night?" she says.

I pull my chin up from my calendar to look at her. Here it comes, another invitation to join her and Hudson for drinks. Natalie seems desperate to play matchmaker for me. She's always trying to get me out for the weekend to meet someone. Of course, I'm doing everything in my power not to have a run-in with Hudson.

"Oh, you know," I say giving her a tight smile. "Just Netflix and chill with my cat."

"Well, Hudson is in town and he has a really cute doctor friend..."

Here we go.

"I appreciate the thought, Natalie, but I'm just not looking to date right now. I had a bad breakup last year and I just need some time alone."

Her face falls. "I know, I know. But if you change your mind..."

"You'll be the first to know."

She shoots me a forced smile before retreating into her office. I turn my focus back to the computer screen in front of me, noticing an email from John has just popped up. It's the contract paperwork for Natalie to sign—the final step in their joint purchase of the apartment complex. I eagerly click print, sending the pages across the office to our shared printer.

I gather up the paperwork, stack it into a neat pile, and knock on Natalie's office door.

"Come in," she says.

"I have some paperwork for you to sign." I walk towards her desk, noticing she has a framed picture of her and Hudson sitting on top. My heart clenches. *That's new.* I drop the stack of papers in front of her with a pen sitting on top.

"What's this for?" she asks cheerfully.

"It's that deal you've been working on with Declan."

"Oh yes, thank you," she says, reaching for the papers. "I've been looking forward to this project. This could be a great opportunity for us, Claire."

Us. Just the way she says it kind of makes me want to throw up in my mouth.

"Nice picture," I say, pointing to the frame. "Is that your boyfriend?"

"Oh yes," she says. "Isn't he handsome? And he's so sweet too. I really hope you get to meet him someday, Claire."

I pull my lips in a tight line. "How long have you been dating?"

"Oh, about a year. But it feels like longer. We have this connection...it's hard to explain. And you mentioned a proposal earlier." Her eyes practically sparkle with glee. "I do think he might propose on our getaway. He's the one, I know it."

I nearly lose my lunch. I pick up the frame. "He is really cute. Has he ever been married before?"

A confused look crosses Natalie's eyes. *I probably shouldn't have asked that.*

"No." She shakes her head. "He said he's had some girl-friends in the past but nothing serious."

I fight with every ounce of self-control not to hurl the frame back onto her desk, shattering it into a million pieces. Hudson stripped me of everything, leaving me humiliated and broken. And to add insult to injury, he refuses to even acknowledge his own marriage?

I have to bite the inside of my cheek just to keep myself in check. I place the frame back on her desk, my hand trembling slightly.

"If you get those papers signed," I say, hoping she doesn't notice the clench in my jaw, "I can get them FedExed back over to Declan this afternoon."

"Of course," she says. "I'll start reading through the contract now."

I nod and carefully make my way out of her office. Once I've gently closed the door, I storm across the hall. I step outside the front door and try to collect myself, letting the afternoon sun burn my skin. I squeeze my eyes closed.

Three weeks. Three weeks until the two of them are on a boat, cruising towards the McDermott mansion.

Romantic getaway? *She has no idea.*

31

ONE WEEK EARLIER

I reach for the door handle of my apartment, juggling bags of wine and carryout from a local Thai restaurant. Just as I am about to open the door, it slides open, revealing a casually dressed John waiting in the doorway. His dark eyebrows are knitted together and a tight expression is on his lips. *He doesn't look happy.*

"You're early," I say, ignoring the stern look on his face by giving him a bright smile.

"I'll take those," he says, pulling the bags from my arms. The tightness of his tone and the way he snatches the bags out of my hands tells me something is definitely up. I sigh. Knowing John, we'll be getting into it shortly. He hasn't exactly been supportive of my plans the last few weeks.

The two of use amble towards the kitchen, where John drops the wine and food on the counter. Gucci saunters into the room, weaving her way through my legs. I pick her up and give her a nuzzle. She purrs loudly.

"Did you give the cat a buzz cut?" he asks.

"Yes," I say, patting her bare belly. "I was worried about fleas."

John arches an eyebrow at the two of us, but says nothing. I had the groomer give her a close shave. Her once fluffy white fur is now a half inch long. It makes her look completely different, which was my goal. I drop her to the ground just before we enter the kitchen. That's when I notice the little surprise I've been working on for Natalie is lying in the center of the island. Which is not where I left it.

Uh-oh. I'm in trouble.

John wastes no time. He picks up the diary and glares at me.

"Care to explain what this little diary is all about?"

I give him a placating smile. Oops, that was a fun little detail I forgot to share with John. I don't say a word, but instead go to the cabinet and pull out two wine glasses.

"I was going to tell you about that. It's a little surprise for Natalie."

"A fake diary? This wasn't part of the plan, Viv."

I pull a wine opener out of the draw and start uncorking the first bottle.

"Let's eat first," I say. He rolls his eyes and starts pulling out some plates from the cabinet. I've enjoyed this part— playing house with John every weekend. I've been able to see him in a different light here, away from our usual spots in Chicago.

Of course, I knew he would be mad about the diary. But I couldn't resist the idea of messing with Natalie. She thinks Hudson is the perfect man. Successful, handsome...and honest.

He's *anything* but honest. And in order to help prove what a liar he is, I crafted this little diary to throw her off-course. I'm not sure how long it will take her to figure out Hudson and JJ are one and the same, but once she does, it will make Hudson look suspicious. Even when she finds out he wasn't married to Tess, she will still have her doubts.

One thing I've learned from being an attorney is that reasonable doubt is everything—and in relationships, trust is everything.

Where there is doubt, trust crumbles like a fragile house of cards.

Besides, once I started writing in my diary, I couldn't stop. It was an exhilarating escape from reality, a way to process my thoughts and emotions without fear of judgment.

My mother? The inheritance? The relationship with Hudson, whom I refer to as JJ?

It's all there. Part autobiography and part fiction.

Even though Dr. Sloan had suggested keeping a diary for years, I never took her seriously until now. But instead of following her well-intentioned advice, I twisted it into something else. A way for me to cast doubt in Natalie's mind about Hudson. Who he really is...not her knight in shining armor, but instead a liar and a cheat.

John takes a slow sip from his wine glass and gives me an impatient expression. He's dressed in a cashmere half-zip sweater and jeans. When I lean over to grab some more noodles, I detect a hint of expensive cologne. I can't help but notice he looks kind of cute. Especially when he's waiting on me. Why do I take so much pleasure in watching him sweat?

"I was just having some fun. That diary will make 'Natalie doubt everything that Hudson has ever told her. She'll think he killed Tess, and that's what we want her to believe." I wrap some noodles around my fork. "Did you know he lied about me? She doesn't even know he was married before."

John cocks his head at me, twirling the wine glass in his hands. "What about when Natalie talks to the police? Tells them how Tess kept a diary claiming that she was married to Hudson? Even though it's not true. It will destroy her credibility, and Tess's too."

I nod, letting a smile spread across my lips. "Is that a bad thing?"

"You're playing with fire."

I take a drink of wine, the cool liquid running down my throat. "I'm having fun."

John rolls his eyes. "With you? One and the same."

I can't resist a laugh. He knows me too well. We eat a few more bites of the Thai noodles in silence.

"Did Tess really push you in the lake?" he asks.

"It was the opposite, actually."

"Geesh," he says, pushing the glasses up on his nose. "You have a unique way of twisting the truth."

I give him a sheepish grin. "I guess I can always write fiction if practicing law doesn't work out."

"I think you should stick to being a lawyer," he says, reaching for the wine bottle and refilling our glasses. "You realize this is evidence of your part in this whole thing."

"The diary will disappear before that becomes an issue."

John shakes his head. "I don't like this, Viv."

I place a hand on his shoulder, feeling the soft cashmere beneath my fingers. "You worry too much."

His eyes bore into mine with a warning glare before he turns back to his food, trying to brush off the issue for now. It's a relief that he trusts me so utterly, but as a lawyer, he should know better than to let his guard down completely.

Men are always too trusting when it comes to women, especially when intimacy is involved. But as a woman, I know better. We are always wary, always cautious, always waiting for the other shoe to drop.

"So you have everything in place? The evidence is ready?"

"Yes, it's ready."

He finishes his plate and carries it to the sink. For the most part, men are easy. Flash a little skin, tease them with a little kiss. Simple. John has been fairly easy to manipulate and I haven't even kissed him yet. Hudson, on the other hand, was not easy. That's probably why I was so obsessed with him. He always kept me on my toes.

I watch John for a moment as he's cleaning the kitchen. I can tell there's something eating at him.

"What is it, John?"

He lets out a sigh. Looks up at me from the sink. "This is just so...risky."

"High risk, high reward," I quip.

"If you say so." He finishes putting his plate in the dishwasher and walks back over to where I'm sitting. "Listen, Vivian, after this we're even, okay? No more favors that involve breaking the law."

"You have my word," I say with a smile. Then I lean over and do something I hadn't planned. I kiss him on the lips. At first he doesn't move, surprised by the gesture. Then he leans in and wraps his arms around me, kissing me hungrily.

As we make our way to the bedroom, I finally decide to give John what he's been silently asking for since law school. Like I said, men tend to be more trusting...especially when they're sleeping with you.

32

THREE DAYS EARLIER

I peek through the fogged glass window of the boathouse, anxiously awaiting Bart's arrival. The thumping of my heart in my ears drowns out every other sound as I watch him approach in that ancient wooden boat with Hudson and Natalie in tow. My stomach has been in knots for days now, holed up on the island, meticulously preparing for the weekend ahead.

I'm not alone. Gucci is here with me. Against John's warnings, I brought her along to keep me company. She's been acting strangely, constantly sniffing and disappearing into the shadows of the property. My nerves are on edge as I struggle to keep her in sight, knowing that she could easily slip away and find Hudson, which would give me away immediately.

Despite months of preparation for this event, there are still numerous details to manage. I had to create a detailed spreadsheet to keep track of everything, which I will be sure to delete entirely by the end of the weekend. If John knew that file even existed, he'd be horrified.

A crucial aspect of my plan is controlling communication. A simple Google search led me to a GPS mobile jammer, a small device roughly the size of a laptop with multiple antennas protruding from it. With just one click, I can effectively block all cell phone signals within a quarter-mile radius, making it the perfect tool for cutting off communication on the island.

Just moments ago, I switched it off when I saw Bart leaving for the docks. I needed to make a phone call pretending to be Claire to Natalie, so I could tell her about an urgent issue with the upcoming deal. And, of course, John's—aka Declan's—sudden disappearance.

My voice quivered with excitement as I left her the voicemail, knowing she'll be sweating bullets as soon as she hears it. I picture the color draining from her carefully made-up face. Deep down she knows she shouldn't have signed away her life savings. But John and I were convincing. We made the offer irresistible.

The boathouse isn't anything to sniff at. A later addition to the estate, it boasts some pretty lavish amenities, a fully-equipped kitchen with top-of-the-line appliances, a bathroom with a massive tub, and a spacious bedroom that overlooks the water—much nicer than the dingy little apartment I used while pretending to be Claire.

Gaining entry to the property was surprisingly simple. I had met Bart, the long-time caretaker, on a few occasions before—namely my wedding day. He was quite willing to let me stay for the weekend in order to keep an eye on Hudson after I told him my theory about Tess's disappearance. I also offered him a sizeable sum of money to turn a blind eye and not mention my name while I hid in the shadows.

With my binoculars pressed to my eyes, I can see Natalie's face contorting in agony as she retches over the side of the boat. A twisted smile spreads across my lips, watching her perfect hair and flawless makeup become disheveled by the merciless seasickness. I couldn't have planned it any better. *Serves her right.*

The two of them make their way off the boat and start walking up to the property. I take a step back into the room, adjusting my binoculars so I can see the two of them. When I see Hudson in the flesh, my heart stops. It's been months since I've actually laid eyes on him. And he looks...so good. When he wraps his hand around Natalie's, I feel my heart breaking all over again.

I'm about to turn the GPS signal blocker back on when my phone buzzes. I look down to see John's number on the caller ID.

"Hey there, handsome," I greet him, swallowing my feelings.

"Hey, Vivian," his voice comes through the phone line. He sounds nervous, despite my repeated assurances that there's nothing to worry about. "So, how's it going?"

"Great! I just left a voicemail for Natalie, explaining that you have suddenly disappeared without a trace. They are walking up the docks now and I'm just about to turn the signal blocker I found back on."

"Are you sure you want to do this?"

John has been questioning my decision every day for the last week. I appreciate his concern, but I've assured him over and over again that everything will work out fine.

"Yes, I'm sure," I say, rolling my eyes.

"You don't have to stay there, you know. You could just jump on a boat and come meet me for drinks at the Moose Lodge. They have penny beers on Tuesdays."

"Sounds delightful," I snort.

John insisted on coming with me and holing up at the local lodge while I execute our plan. He also helped me find a reliable exit strategy.

Tucked below me in the boat garage is a deep-V hull boat with a massive engine on the back that will slice through any rough water. The nice old man we rented it from told me it's the same boat the Coast Guard uses. Definitely not as stylish as the vintage wood boat that Bart brought the guests in on, but it doesn't make anyone seasick either.

"Seriously, you'd be better off here, with me."

The way he's asking tells me everything I need to know. I haven't forgotten about our recent tryst. Yet, John of all people should know not to get in my way.

"And miss the look on Hudson's face when I tell him he's going to jail? No way."

There is a moment of silence on the other line. "Just be careful, Viv."

"Always," I say and hang up the phone.

I lower my binoculars just in time to see Gucci strolling towards the door. I suddenly remember Bart lived here with his little dog for a time. While he was here, he installed a doggie door, which was now partly open. I should have locked it when we arrived. Before I can even call her back, Gucci has slipped through the door and out into the yard.

"Gucci!" I call after her anxiously. Even with her new buzz cut, there is a chance Hudson may recognize her. He never really cared much for the cat, but Gucci might remember him too.

I quickly put on my boots and chase after her, trying to stay hidden. That cat is surprisingly fast. She darts across the landscaped yard and disappears behind the back of the house. I follow cautiously, staying hidden among the tall cypress trees that have been carefully landscaped around the property.

I catch a glimpse of Natalie's silhouette turning towards me. My heart catches in my throat. I quickly dive out of sight, my breathing ragged as I lean up against a tree.

That was close.

I know exactly where Gucci is going. She's been really interested in the basement of the property, which I'm guessing is full of mice, just waiting to be captured. I've had to pull her out of there more than once.

I check the keys in my pocket. Part of my agreement with Bart was to have all the keys to the property, not just the boathouse. There's a side entrance back by the butler's pantry near the kitchen. Earlier today I snuck inside to set the stage for a few items, specifically a Monopoly board game that I know Hudson wouldn't be able to resist. When I saw the gorgeous spread of food and wine Bart had left for them in the living room, I felt indignant...and then gleefully helped myself to a glass of champagne.

After a brisk run around the house, I take a deep breath and slowly turn the doorknob back, trying to keep the creaking sound to a minimum.

The sounds of Hudson and Natalie climbing the stairs reaches my ears. In my head, I picture Natalie walking towards the master closet, where I have purposely left the diary inside the limited-edition green Gucci purse she had been pining for. I didn't feel one bit of guilt on the day she asked me to go buy it for her and I swiped it for myself instead. It would make the perfect bait. I knew she wouldn't be able to stop herself from picking up the purse and peering inside.

I lick my lips. *I hope she enjoys my little story.*

Once the footsteps have faded away, I cautiously pad down to the basement. To say this basement is creepy is an understatement. Apparently Tess's grandfather was a prolific hunter who liked to display his trophies. The walls are lined with an eerie display of taxidermy animals, ranging from deer and bears to smaller creatures like birds and squirrels. The air is thick with a musty scent of fur and mold, making me want to hold my breath.

In the dim light, I spot Gucci crouched in the corner, her green eyes gleaming with anticipation. She's on the hunt.

"Not today, Gucci," I say, scooping her up in my arms. She jumps out of my hands and lands on the floor, knocking over a petrified squirrel with a loud bang.

I freeze for few seconds, listening for footsteps. To my relief, nothing happens.

"Gucci, come here," I say in a harsh whisper. She gives me a guilty look then runs and jumps in my arms.

With Gucci gently cradled, I carefully climb the stairs towards the kitchen. Just as I am about to slip out unnoticed, I hear moans and grunts coming from the upstairs bedroom.

The sound of the two of them going at it is enough to make my stomach turn. But I know their love will soon come crashing down, and the thought fills me with a sick satisfaction.

33

TWO DAYS EARLIER

The following morning, I open my eyes at 5 a.m., fully awake. Moving around the house in the dark without turning on any lights is a bit of a challenge, but I don't want to risk the two of them seeing any light coming from the boathouse. After fumbling my way through the darkness, I manage to make coffee in the bathroom with the door closed and the lights on. Then, I grab some smoked salmon and a bagel from the fridge for breakfast.

As I take a bite of my breakfast, my eyes wander out the window and catch sight of Hudson running on the property. I immediately plaster myself against the wall, careful that he doesn't spot me through the window. My heart pounds against my ribcage. Flashbacks of the last time I saw him running here flood my mind.

Our wedding day.

Hudson and I were married on this very island. After we found out I was 'pregnant' we had to put together a wedding rather quickly. Tess immediately offered up her place as the perfect private spot for a small and intimate wedding. A famous event planner from New York flew in and put the whole event together in just a few weeks' time. It was just as I described in the diary...breathtakingly beautiful. Better than anything I ever could've imagined.

With one big exception. *Tess.* The part I didn't include in the diary was the way that Hudson and Tess were acting towards each other during the reception.

Everything was going flawlessly, up until the end of our first dance. I relished the attention of our guests when all eyes were on Hudson and me...and Hudson only had eyes for me. We glided across the dance floor, my white silk gown brushing against the parquet floor while the evening lights twinkled around us.

But as the night wore on, we were slowly pulled apart by our friends who were eager to dance and revel in the festivities. I watched as Hudson and Tess, whose dress was cut so low it barely covered her nipples, twirled and spun on the dance floor, showcasing some signature moves they had perfected in college. Soon after, they made their way to the bar where they both did a shot of tequila, a tradition that had carried over from our college days.

Hudson practically undressed her with his eyes, triggering a primal surge of jealousy within me. Tess shamelessly basked in the attention, completely oblivious to the pain she was causing me. Her boyfriend, Scott, sat alone at the bar drowning his sorrows in alcohol, his eyes never leaving them.

As the night wore on and drinks flowed freely, my simmering anger erupted into a violent confrontation. I couldn't ignore how Hudson's desire for her oozed from his every pore, and his denials only added fuel to the fire. It was clear he had either slept with her or desperately wanted to. The mere thought sent me into a frenzy. I spat out accusations and insults, our marriage crumbling before it had hardly even started.

Hudson managed to end the fight by making one key point: he was marrying me, not Tess. However, it planted a seed of doubt. Hudson was the man of my dreams—I was madly in love with him, obsessed even. Was the feeling mutual? It made me wonder if Tess was the one he really wanted to be with.

What if I hadn't gotten 'pregnant'? He might have preferred to marry her instead.

I know it would be a few minutes before he made it back to the house after his run, so I decide to sneak into the house and find a spot from where I can spy on the two of them. I want to see if Natalie has found Tess's diary and if she's secretly reading it.

I make my way up to the main house and walk in through the back door. There's a tiny mudroom and utility closet tucked behind the kitchen, and so I hide away in the closet. I flick off the GPS cell phone signal jammer for the moment, just making sure that Natalie has a chance to listen to my message.

Then I patiently wait for his return.

A few minutes later, I hear the sound of plates, and food being pulled out of the refrigerator. Hudson has always loved to cook and I imagine he's pulling together a delicious breakfast. My mouth waters as the sizzle of bacon hits the pan. When the sound of Frank Sinatra floats into the closet, I clench my jaw.

Sinatra and cooking. Signature Hudson. I used to love that about him.

I hear Natalie enter the room and listen closely as the two of them talk. Has it hit her yet? That every bit of her precious nest egg of money is gone? If not, it will soon.

And once Hudson finds out she has to file for bankruptcy? He'll dump her in a heartbeat. He already took a financial hit from our divorce; I made sure of that. He can't afford another messy breakup. But to my surprise Natalie doesn't mention anything about the diary or the phone calls she received. Smart girl. She's waiting for the right moment.

Looks like Hudson's not the only one keeping secrets in this relationship.

Confident I've heard enough for now, I pry open the door and stroll to the exit. As I sneak around the corner, I catch sight of something that makes my heart stop...

The two of them locked together in a rocking motion on top of the kitchen island. Natalie's bare legs are wrapped around his waist as he thrusts himself into her. I freeze for a moment, staring in horror at the two of them having sex... right in the same place where...I shake my head.

Don't go there, Vivian. Don't even think about that right now.

The pressure building inside me suddenly breaks, like a fragile twig snapping underfoot. The urge to scream rises up, but I bite down hard on my lip and make a mad dash towards the back door. *Hudson is mine. My husband. The man I married, right here on this island.*

My heart hammers in my chest as I fumble with the doorknob, desperate to escape the suffocating atmosphere inside. The cool air hits my face as I burst outside, finally able to take a deep, cleansing breath. The world around me seems to blur as I stumble away from the house, my mind consumed with a whirlwind of emotions and thoughts.

I can't believe it. I can't believe Hudson could be so cruel. How can he do this to me? *Over and over.*

I meant it when I told John that I would let it go after this was all over. But now? The rage I feel...the fury of injustice... I don't think I will ever be able to let it go. Some wounds are too deep to ever heal.

When I'm safely behind the locked door of the boathouse, I run to the bathroom and throw up in the toilet. Again and again. My hands tremble as I hold onto the sides of the seat. After my entire breakfast has exited my body, I slide back onto the cool tile floor, my body trembling. Gucci makes her way to me, rubbing against my arm with a soft purr.

I'm suddenly exhausted, but I manage to find my way to the bedroom, where I curl up in a ball and fall fast asleep.

THE SOUND of someone rattling the front door jolts me awake. I quickly look for a place to hide, my eyes landing on the closet in the corner. I grab Gucci and leap into the closet, shutting the door behind us. In the darkness, my heart pounds against the walls of my chest. I hold my breath, willing myself to stay silent and still. Every creak and groan of the boathouse feels like an explosion in my ears.

I hear voices; they start off close by, but then fade into the distance. It seems that Hudson and Natalie have decided to sneak into the boathouse for some reason, but now they've left.

Curious, I work my way to the front door. Outside the window, I can see the two of them walking back to the house. Hudson has his arm around her. She's wobbling slightly. That's when I notice the dark red patches on her arm and leg.

She's bleeding.

Suddenly the sky opens up and it begins to pour down on the two of them. Hudson nearly slips and falls. Gucci runs through my legs and out the door, following them towards the house. I take a few quick steps towards the door.

Whatever is going on, I'll find out soon enough.

34

PRESENT DAY

I stand in the rain with my back shoved uncomfortably up against a large pine tree. I would give anything for an umbrella right now, but I can't risk being seen by Hudson at this point. It's nearly dark outside. The rain clouds have choked out the late afternoon sun.

I spent the entire day packing up everything in the boathouse, including Gucci.

My sweet little cat was reluctant to get inside her crate, but eventually I was able to lure her in with some treats. I tucked her into the carrier crate, and dropped her on the dock next to the boat I have rented for my escape.

My plan is deceptively simple, although it took me months to carefully map out each step. In order for the police to convict Hudson of Tess's murder, I need to have a pretty convincing case. I remember one of my professors in law school used to say, "A case is like a puzzle—the more pieces you have, the clearer the picture." In the case of Tess's murder, I plan to paint a crystal-clear picture that includes motive, means, opportunity and, of course, *evidence.*

The motive is rather simple; the bit about Tess leaving Hudson money in her will is actually true. Using my connections from law school, I was able to figure out who Tess used as her estate attorney. I was lucky enough to know one of the lawyers at the firm, and he managed to give me access to her files because I was acting on behalf of my husband. Seeing the will confirmed that Hudson was named as a beneficiary. Still, I was stunned when I found out. There was his name, *Hudson Jenkins*, with a nice little sum of money reserved just for him.

A set of text messages between the two of them, which I found on her phone later, served as further motive. In those messages, Hudson had made it clear that he was worried about their brief affair becoming public knowledge. He asked Tess to keep quiet about it.

So, if I was arguing this case in court, I would state that Hudson was clearly motivated by a 'deadly' combination of money and a need for silence. Believe me, after studying case law, I've seen people commit murder for less.

As for the means and opportunity, I have an eyewitness, Bart, who can place him on the island the weekend Tess disappeared. Don't let that charming Scottish accent fool you—Bart was eager to make a little extra cash in exchange for his testimony. In fact, for an extra sum, he let me in on a little secret: Hudson bribed him to keep quiet about his visit to the island the weekend Tess disappeared. Which means the police never even knew he was here. I was furious when he told me.

But every lie he told only cemented my desire for justice.

Couple Bart's statement with travel records and receipts, and there would be no doubt that Hudson was here with Tess on the day she was murdered.

But the pièce de résistance of my conviction will be none other than a blood-stained knife. It may seem cliché, but I already possess the murder weapon, its blade coated in dried and crusted blood from Tess's lifeless body. All that remains is to transfer Hudson's fingerprints onto the handle and then strategically place it in plain sight for the authorities to discover. The weight of the knife in my backpack sends shivers down my spine as I imagine the satisfaction of seeing Hudson pay for his crimes.

Once I have that little piece of evidence in place, I plan on Gucci and I making a swift exit from the island. There is a fully gassed speed boat tied up inside the boathouse. Because the door of the boat garage is closed, Hudson and Natalie had no idea that a fully capable boat was ready and able to take them to shore.

But now comes the tricky part. The part that I've been steeling myself for over the last few weeks. I need to confront Hudson face to face. And that won't be easy. Months of building up courage could all crumble when we come face to face, but I have no choice. I need to face him. *I won't leave this island without some sort of closure.*

The rain pounds relentlessly against my face as I squint through the darkness, the sporadic flashes of lightning illuminating the front door. Bart's old wool cap shields my eyes from the downpour, but my heart races as I await any sign of movement. My breath hitches when I finally catch a glimpse of Hudson's frame emerging from the front door, his determined stride cutting through the storm. He probably thinks he can get a signal and try to reach out for help. Actually, I'm counting on it. He has no idea the GPS signal jammer in my backpack makes that impossible.

If it had been a few hours earlier, the situation would

have been different. I had disabled the signal jammer so that I could quickly make a call to Natalie, pretending to be Claire. The memory of her voice wavering and on the brink of tears brings me a sense of satisfaction. In my guise as Claire, I informed her that someone had taken out a loan in her name for $500,000. Of course, this is all a lie; there is no loan. But the documents I sent to her are convincing enough to make her believe she would be on the hook for the money. And if that were true, she knows her life would be ruined. She would have to declare bankruptcy and lose everything she has worked hard to build. The thought of this brings warmth to my stomach. After I completed the call, I flipped the cell phone jammer back on, the position that it is now.

So when Hudson makes his exit out the door, I know that his attempts to contact anyone for help will be futile. I watch as Hudson fades into the rain. I leave my cover of the tree and walk about ten yards up to the side of the house where I've been sneaking into the kitchen. My backpack is loaded with a variety of supplies that I'll need for the evening, including zip ties, a gun, and a bottle of chloral hydrate.

I stumbled upon the idea of using chloral hydrate while binge-watching true crime documentaries and eating ice cream late at night. A small dose is enough to render someone unconscious, but too much could put them in a coma. It was the perfect solution for getting Hudson's fingerprints on the knife without risking getting caught. Knocking him out would make things a lot simpler for me.

I proposed the plan to drug Hudson to John, but he was hesitant. He pointed out some potential flaws, like the risk of overdosing and killing him, which would create a whole new set of problems. I shrugged off his concerns, confident that I could find a dosage that would just knock him out without causing any permanent harm. John reached out to a contact who could provide us with the necessary medication. Now, all that's left is to plant it in a spot where Hudson will take it willingly.

This is where the advantage of having been married to him before comes in handy. He's always been one to drink lots of water, especially when stressed. It's almost like a nervous habit for him. So, I quietly work my way to the kitchen and grab a few glasses, filling them with water and adding precisely two drops of the drug to each one. Based on my research, this should be enough for what I have planned. Once they're ready, I leave one glass in the kitchen and tiptoe into the living room.

To my relief, the room is deserted. I walk on my toes, careful to make no noise. Despite my efforts, droplets from my rain-soaked coat fall onto the floor, leaving behind a small trail. But I doubt anyone will notice. A deafening clap of thunder rattles the windows, sending shockwaves through the house. My grip tightens around the glass as I struggle to hold on, feeling its weight threaten to slip from my trembling fingers. I manage to carefully lower it onto the coffee table.

I retrace my steps back into the kitchen, quietly placing my backpack in the pantry. A sense of unease washes over me as I think about Gucci huddled next to the boat. Hopefully Hudson didn't happen to go into the boat garage. I decide it's best I double-check. I reach in my bag and grab my gun, feeling its weight in my hand. My heart races as I steel myself for what might come next. With a swift motion, I pull my cap down low over my eyes before venturing out into the storm.

As I step outside, the howling wind whips against my

face and stings my skin. The rain pours down in sheets, drenching me within seconds. In the distance, I catch sight of Hudson through the thick curtain of rain, about twenty yards away. He spots me at the same time and our eyes lock for a split second before I quickly duck behind a nearby tree, trying to hide from his view.

"Hello? Hello." His words cut through the howling wind. "Vivian? Is that you?"

The sound of my name from his lips sends a shock through my body, stirring up all the feelings and memories from our past. My heart races and I press myself tighter against the tree, not daring to move or speak for several minutes.

When I finally gather the courage to look, Hudson is nowhere in sight. He must have gone back inside to talk to Natalie. I give up my plan to check on Gucci and the boat and make my way back indoors. It's only a matter of time before Hudson falls unconscious, and I don't want to waste my chance to get his fingerprints on the knife.

Besides, it's high time Hudson and I have a little chat.

35

Breathless and cramped, I stand in the small pantry, my arms trembling from dragging Hudson's limp body across the expansive living room and into the kitchen. My hands sweat inside the black plastic gloves I'm wearing to keep my fingerprints from appearing all over the house.

I can't let Natalie see me. *Not yet.*

The weight of his muscular frame, all one hundred and eighty pounds of it, feels like a ton of bricks in my arms. Each step is a struggle as I navigate through cluttered shelves and stray boxes, praying that she won't hear me. When I finally make it to the pantry and close the door, I let out a long breath.

The chloral hydrate worked like a charm. For a moment, I worried that he would pass out in front of Natalie. But as she stormed away in frustration, I exhaled with relief. His eyes drooped, heavy with the tranquilizing effects of the drug. He stared at his hands for a moment and then slumped forward, landing on the couch with a thud.

Ugh. Just listening to their conversation made me feel sick. Hearing Hudson tell her what happened from his point of view...makes it sound like he never loved me at all. And calling me mentally unstable? That is totally unfair. It was all I could do to stay in the shadows and bite my tongue. He only told Natalie part of the story about the pregnancy, conveniently leaving out what happened afterwards and what he's keeping from her—and kept from me.

I listen through the sounds of the storm, trying to hear Natalie's footsteps.

"Hudson?" Natalie's quivering voice cuts through. "Hudson, where are you?"

The rhythmic thud of Natalie's footsteps echoes through the living room and kitchen, creating a sense of unease in the quiet house. I tense up, anticipating her arrival at the door, but I've already made sure to lock it from the inside. A sense of relief washes over me as I realize she won't be able to enter. Hudson sleeps peacefully at my feet, his breathing so quiet I worry he might not wake up. Hopefully I didn't put too many drops of the chloral hydrate in his glass of water.

Natalie's footsteps continue to move around, coming closer and then receding again.

"Hudson, wherever you are," she calls out to an empty house, "I'm taking the boat and I'm leaving."

I can't help but smile. *Good luck with that, Natalie.*

The stairs creak as she ascends towards the top floor, leaving us alone on the main floor for now. While she packs her bags, I unzip the backpack I brought with me. I feel around in the dim light for the pack of zip ties and duct tape.

After a few moments, the sound of Natalie's footsteps echoes down the stairs, her heavy suitcase hitting the banister as she makes her way to the front door. When she opens it the rumble of the storm echoes inside the house. Then, I hear the loud click of the door closing behind her, signaling that Hudson and I are finally alone. The only sounds now are the distant roars of thunder and our own breathing.

With a quick twist of the doorknob, I fling open the closet door and take a deep breath. I was starting to get a little claustrophobic. I drag Hudson's body across the kitchen and into the dining room and carefully prop him up in a chair. Working quickly, I pull out my pack of zip ties and start securing his arms and legs to the chair one by one. I double up the ties, just in case he's strong enough to break through them.

I fumble around in the backpack for the bottle of smelling salts. For a moment, it occurs to me that I might have taken things too far. *Zip ties and smelling salts?* It's like something out of a movie. But I try to remember that this wasn't just my idea. John helped me come up with this too. Granted, we were a little drunk at the time, but he still managed to purchase all of these supplies for me without detection.

And of course, after listening to Hudson's nauseating conversation with Natalie? *He deserves what's coming to him.*

I shove the small vial of smelling salts under his nose, the pungent scent instantly filling the air around us. He slowly starts to stir. After what feels like an eternity, his eyelids flutter open and he looks around with a dazed expression. As our eyes meet, his widen in recognition and his mouth falls open slightly. His pupils dilate, revealing a mixture of surprise and fear at seeing me there.

He jerks in his seat, straining against the zip ties.

"Vivian," he says, his voice raspy. "What in the hell is going on?"

I pull over a chair from the dining table and take a seat across from him.

"I thought we might have a little chat," I say, rocking back into the seat and crossing my legs. He yanks at the ties again, realizing he won't be able to break them. After a couple of seconds of effort, he lets his arms go slack.

"This is insane. Untie me now, Vivian," he says, glaring at me.

I shake my head. "I can't do that."

"Why?"

"Like I said, we need to talk."

Hudson opens his mouth to speak, then closes it. He opens it again. I can see the wheels turning in his head as he is trying to figure out how he can talk himself out of this.

"I'm all ears," he says.

I let out a dramatic sigh. "Well, I've decided it's time for you to pay for all the crimes you've committed against me."

"Crimes?" he says, eyebrows raised.

"Maybe crime is too strong a word. How about lying to me, cheating on me? Ruining my life?"

Hudson rolls his eyes. "I already paid fifty thousand dollars for that," he says, practically spitting out the words. "Remember that little lifestyle clause you put in our prenup?"

I nod. "Yes, and I do appreciate your payment. I made sure to donate it to a good cause. But it just doesn't feel like enough. I mean, you cheated on me more than once."

He shakes his head. "No, I didn't."

"Liar," I say, pointing my finger into his chest. It's hard for me to restrain myself, listening to all of his lies. I want to reach across the space between us and smack him across the face. *It won't help you feel any better,* I keep telling myself.

"What do you want me to say, Vivian? It's over. It's been over for six months. You need to move on!"

I shrug my shoulders, using every bit of willpower I possess to retain my composure. "That's what everyone keeps telling me," I say, feeling the rage inside my belly. "I just don't think it's fair. It's not fair that you get to move on and live happily ever after now that you have destroyed our marriage."

"I destroyed our marriage? You lied to me first." He rolls his eyes at me. "Wake up, Vivian. We got a divorce. It happens all the time."

"Not to me, it doesn't," I say defiantly. "Don't you get it, Hudson? You took away...all of my firsts. My first engagement. My first wedding. I'll never wear white again without thinking of the moment we shared on this island. That's what you destroyed, my innocence."

I fight back tears, the last few words catching in my throat. Hudson struggles in his seat again, trying to move. It's useless.

"So what are you going to do, Vivian?" he says, his eyes boring into mine. "Have you tied me up so you can torture me? Do you think that will make you feel better about everything that happened?"

His words feel like a punch to the gut. "Actually, now that you mention it, that's not a bad idea," I say. "Torture. But I don't really have the stomach for blood, like you do."

He gives me a curious look, but I continue. "No, I have something better in mind."

In the dimly lit room, he squints at me, attempting to intimidate me with his stare. But I can see the fear in his eyes, the way his complexion has paled. He's afraid of me, and for the first time, I feel a sense of power...and complete control.

It's exhilarating, having the upper hand over him, being able to have the final say. I want to savor this moment forever, hold onto it tightly.

Because Hudson is finally mine and I can do whatever I want with him.

PART III

SHOWDOWN

36

NATALIE

"Hudson? Hudson, where are you?"

I don't understand. He was just here.

The lack of light makes each room feel like a maze, and for a moment I'm afraid I might get lost. The living room is eerily silent. When I arrive in the kitchen, a flash of thunder lights up the room, revealing every corner, but no one's inside. I make my way to the dining room, my footsteps echoing loudly against the cold wood floor, sending chills down my spine.

But there is no trace of him. Panic tightens its grip on my chest, each breath coming harder as I realize I'm alone in this big mansion. Or maybe not alone. Both options feel terrifying.

Outside, the storm rages on with relentless fury, beating against the windows like an angry mob. The deafening sound reverberates throughout the house, amplifying my fear. I huddle into myself, feeling small and helpless.

I decide to make one more lap and descend into the dimly lit basement. My hand scrambles along the wall in a desperate search for the light switch, but when I finally find it and flip it on, nothing happens. My heart plummets—the power must have gone out again. I can only stand in the taxidermy-filled room for a few seconds before returning to the main floor.

It's painfully evident that Hudson has taken off and left me stranded, without a glance back or a second thought. I don't need to waste any more time searching for him. He has made his choice, and now I need to make mine.

"Hudson, wherever you are," I call out, "I'm taking the boat and I'm leaving."

My heart pounding, I run back up the stairs to our room to gather my things. With the storm outside and a potential stranger in the house, I don't have much time—I need to be strategic about what I pack. I grab just one suitcase and fill it with whatever I can fit, leaving behind the rest. I'll replace it later.

As I zip up my suitcase and pull up the handle, I take one last look at the empty room. Lying on the bed is the diary. The diary that belonged to Tess McDermott.

Or perhaps it belonged to someone else. I'm suddenly not sure. Hudson claims he was never married to Tess. If that's true, then why would someone write a fake diary, pretending to be someone they're not? It really makes no sense. Either the author of the diary is lying, or Hudson is lying.

I really don't know whom to trust, especially now that Hudson has admitted he lied to me. Even though technically it was a lie of omission. Did I ask him if he was married when we met? No. He didn't wear a wedding band so I assumed he was single. And we never really discussed past relationships either. I mean, we were both in our thirties, so I assumed he'd had a serious girlfriend before, but I never pried. I thought if it was important enough to him, he'd tell me about it.

I guess I was wrong. I should have asked more questions.

I finger the handle of my suitcase, debating whether or not to bring the diary with me. An hour ago I was determined to hand it over to the police, give them some much-needed evidence so they could solve the mystery of Tess's disappearance.

Now I'm not so sure.

A loud clap of thunder shakes the room. I turn my head towards the door. I'm not going to find any more answers on this wretched island. I'll let the police find the diary themselves.

I drag the suitcase down the stairs, which makes a loud, thumping noise as it rattles against the railing. One of the banisters snaps as my suitcase hits it at the wrong angle. I glance at the splintered wood as the sound reverberates through the house.

I turn around and keep going. Hudson can cover the damages. I don't care. Besides, I don't have any money left at this point. The thought of walking into my office on Monday morning suddenly seems unbearable. How am I going to explain to the bank that I have no money? What proof do I have that I didn't take out the loan?

Claire said the paperwork was notarized. To be honest, I sign so many papers on a daily basis I could have easily signed it without knowing. Claire usually reads through the paperwork for me and then gives me a summary before signing. I honestly can't remember her saying anything about a bank loan over the last few months.

As I reach the bottom floor of the house, another question gnaws at me. Why did Declan do it? Steal all my money and leave me to face bankruptcy?

The easy answer is greed. Pure and simple greed. *It has to be.* But it still feels like there's something I'm missing.

As I reach the front door I think I hear a sound coming from the kitchen. I hesitate for a moment, trying to decide if I should make one last attempt to find Hudson. I shake my head. It's probably just Gucci sneaking around the house again.

"Goodbye, kitty," I whisper quietly.

I pull open the door, which swings heavily into the room. The wind whips viciously around my body, throwing back my jacket. As soon as the heavy rain starts smashing water against my face, I regret my decision. I reach down and grab the black umbrella that Hudson left propped up by the front door. My arm throbs with the effort of keeping it open against the gusting wind.

I know this is my best option. I can't stay here a second longer looking for Hudson, or wait to be assaulted by whoever has been stalking us on this island.

The door slams behind me with an ominous click as I step outside. I clutch my umbrella tightly against my chest, treating it like a weapon, and make my way down the steep hill. The docks are just ahead, about thirty yards away, and I carefully navigate the slippery path towards them. The rainstorm is unrelenting, making it difficult to see where I'm going. But I press on, my determination outweighing my fear.

As I get closer, I see the boat rocking violently in the water. Memories of my motion sickness on the trip here flood back to me. I know I have to find a way to brave the waters again, even if it means pushing myself to the brink. I take a deep breath and keep going.

As I approach the rocky shoreline, my fingers fumble to unlock my phone and check for a signal. Suddenly, a gust of wind flips my umbrella inside out, sending it sailing across the island. I watch helplessly as it lands in the lake, leaving me fully exposed to the pelting rain. Water soaks through my clothes and hair, and I curse myself for not bringing a raincoat.

I peer down at my phone. *Still no signal.* We're in a complete dead zone.

I look back at the violently rocking boat with a new sense of purpose. I know it's my only chance to get out of here. The shoreline of the mainland is barely visible in the distance, but in between sheets of rain, I can make out a few small lights. It's enough to give me a sliver of hope.

I take a deep breath. I only have one shot at this, so I need to summon all of my remaining strength and make it count.

37

NATALIE

Each step down the slick and rain-drenched dock feels like a precarious balancing act. My suitcase threatens to slip from my grip with each unsteady step, but I refuse to let it fall into the murky water below. Finally, after several close calls and a few falls to my knees, I reach the small fishing boat at the end of the dock. As I peer inside, relief floods through me. The keys are lodged in the ignition.

However, any sense of safety is quickly replaced by dread as I take in the battered aluminum hull and four worn seats inside. At the front of the boat, a chair is mounted, bobbing up and down with the boat. I'm guessing this fishing boat belonged to Bart, as it looks too basic to be part of the estate owner's collection.

A few years ago, I went out on a first date with a guy in Atlanta. He was an avid fisherman and insisted on taking me out on the water. Compared to the size of Flathead Lake, it was like floating on a pond. Which is part of the reason I wasn't expecting to get so sick on our way here. Anyway, he showed me the ropes—how to hook the fish, cast the line. He even let me drive the boat. He was a nice guy, but there was no chemistry between us. But now I hope I can draw upon that experience and figure out how to pilot this thing across the water.

I struggle to lift my suitcase off the dock and toss it into the boat. It lands on the floor with a loud thud. I almost lose my balance in the process, but I grab onto one of the dock pylons to steady myself. The bow of the boat is violently rocking up and down, but I manage to catch it at just the right moment and clumsily make my way inside. There are two ropes—one at the front and one at the back—keeping the boat attached to the dock. It takes some effort, and a few instances of my fingers getting caught, but I eventually unhook them from the dock.

I cautiously lower myself into the worn, cracked leather of the captain's seat. My heart races with anticipation as I grab the key in the ignition and give it a twist. The old boat sputters and coughs, its engine struggling to come to life. With a sinking feeling, I try again, hoping for a different result. But on the third try, and to my relief, the boat finally roars to life, its motor rumbling behind me.

My hands tremble as I scan the unfamiliar controls, desperately trying to recall the boat training I received on my date. A handle catches my eye, and with a shaky grip I pull it back for reverse, praying that I remembered correctly. The boat lurches out of the slip, and with a surge of adrenaline I turn the steering wheel and push the handle forward. As the dark waters churn beneath me, doubts flood my mind.

What was I thinking coming out here alone? Suddenly, a life jacket catches my attention and I reach down and pull it over my shoulders. I let go of the steering wheel for a moment as I fumble with the buckles, which makes the boat sweep left and nearly collide with the dock.

I reach out and grab the steering wheel with my left hand, which sends a rush of pain up my arm. I manage to get it centered before snapping together the last buckle. I adjust the life jacket.

At the very least, I won't drown.

I push the engine back to full throttle, and it lurches forward in the water. A small feeling of relief floods over me.

I'm going to make it. I'm going to get off this ridiculous island and somehow make it to land. In fact, I can see lights from the shoreline off into the distance. It's not really that far. Or at least it looks that way.

A few moments later, the rumbles cough and then stop.

All the thrill of my escape leaves my body. I turn the ignition two, three, four times.

Nothing. I looked down at the gauges. To my utter disappointment, the cause of the engine dying becomes crystal clear.

The boat is out of gas.

At that point, I just start crying; sobbing is more like it. This was intentional. Someone emptied the gas tank on purpose. Probably the same person who has been stalking us on the island. And the same person that left me the mysterious Monopoly card.

Someone hates me, most likely wants to hurt me. And I have no idea why.

I stare at the blackness around me. I am now floating helplessly in the middle of choppy waters, rain pouring down on me in a relentless torrent. My mind scrambles to find a solution, a way to get the boat back to shore. Adrenaline courses through my veins, a primal instinct urging me to survive. I look around frantically, searching for an oar or something to get the boat moving again. Then, I see the boat house in the distance, propped up on the island, promising shelter from the rain.

The realization lands on me with a sudden weight—there's only one way out of this. I turn towards the dark water, feeling a wave of fear wash over me. A single thought repeats in my head, causing my stomach to churn.

I'm going to have to swim for it.

38

VIVIAN

"We were married here, Hudson, right on this island," I say as I stare down at him, my voice trembling with rage and hurt. His body writhes against his restraints. He's desperately trying to break free. The storm rages outside, pounding against the windows as we sit in the abandoned house.

"How could you bring her here?" I continue, watching him struggle. "To the place where we said our vows? Don't you think that was a little bit cruel?"

His expression softens, and for a moment I see a flicker of the man I once loved. But just as quickly, his face hardens, a sneer spreading across his mouth.

"Cruel? You think that's cruel? What do you call this?" He sweeps his gaze over his tied-up limbs. "When are you going to get it into your head, Vivian? Everything that's happened between us is in the past."

My hands tremble with anger, but I manage to restrain myself from reaching out and choking him. He glares up at me as he struggles against the ties. Tears threaten to make their way to my eyes, but I refuse to let them fall. I refuse to give him the satisfaction of seeing me cry.

"You think you can just go through life lying to everyone you meet? Sleeping with any woman that catches your eye? And think it's all in the past, easily dismissed?" I lean closer, my voice dripping with venom. "It doesn't work like that. I won't let you get away with any of this. And Natalie isn't off the hook either."

"What did Natalie ever do to you?" he says.

A single lock of his hair falls into his face, obscuring his view. The urge to reach out and sweep it away tugs at my resolve, but now it's tainted with a seething rage that makes me want to grab a knife and slice it off. Time is a cruel thing, turning what was once pure love into a boiling cauldron of resentment. Every little gesture that used to hold so much meaning now only serves to fuel the anger towards the person I once adored.

"Natalie, the real estate bimbo? Oh, she's done plenty. Starting with sleeping with a married man," I say, glaring at him. If John were here, he'd gently remind me that we set the two of them up. But it doesn't matter. Hudson took the bait, and he did so quickly. It was clear he was ready to move on.

Hudson shakes his head. "She didn't know, Vivian."

I point a finger in his face and note that it's trembling slightly. "That's right, Hudson. She didn't know—because you didn't tell her. Just one of the many lies that you told to both of us."

Hudson looks at me, dark anger rising to his cheeks. "What are you talking about, Vivian?"

I have waited for this moment for over a year. The anger has simmered inside me, fueling my every move, every decision, every thought. And now, as I stand in front of him, I can feel it boiling to the surface. It is time to make him admit what he did to me.

"I'm talking about what else happened here, on this island."

"You already brought that up, Viv." Hearing him use my nickname makes me cringe. "We were married on the island. Blah, blah, blah. I know. I was also here, remember?"

I grind my teeth and let out a breath, trying to calm my racing heart.

"Oh no, Hudson, there's much more that happened on this island. Something that was happening even after you met Natalie and started sleeping with her."

I can see it on his face now, the realization dawning on him. I walk around the room, taking in every detail, savoring this moment of anticipation. I run my fingers along the smooth, polished wood of the dining table, tracing the carving around the edge.

About a year ago, I was going through what you might call a rough time. I started drinking a lot more and sleeping with whoever the lucky guy happened to be at the bar that night. I was angry, confused. I didn't understand how Hudson could jump in bed with someone else so quickly. Sure, I set him up with Natalie, but we were only separated at the time. We hadn't even had our first divorce hearing yet.

And what's worse was that my entire reputation was on the line. Once our group of friends from college found out what happened between us, I would go from being seen as a successful lawyer to a crazy, desperate ex-wife. That is, unless I was able to tell my side of the story first—that Hudson cheated on me, which was the real reason behind our divorce. After that little tidbit of news started floating around, and people found out I had proof, all his credibility would be gone.

So I flew out here to Montana to meet with Tess in person. More than anyone I knew, Tess loved a juicy bit of gossip. I pictured us drinking fine wine and eating delicious finger foods while I laid out the entire demise of our marriage. After that, it would only be few days before everyone we knew heard what a bastard Hudson was and how he cheated on me. Of course, I told John it was a 'girls' weekend'. He didn't know the extent of my plan.

My plan was straightforward, yet I knew it would be effective. During my flight to the island, I felt a sense of calm wash over me, as if the weight of my ruined reputation had already been lifted.

But when I arrived, something unthinkable happened.

I made my way through the choppy waters in a rented boat taxi, the anticipation of surprising her building with each passing wave. The boat eventually dropped me off at the dock, and I made my way up to the house. As I approached the front door and knocked, my excitement turned to confusion when no one answered. Not wanting to give up just yet, I decided to take a walk around the side of the house to see if Tess was home.

As I made my way around the house, my eyes caught sight of the kitchen window. What I saw nearly stopped my heart. The image of that day burned itself into my brain, searing into my memory like a brand. In that moment, a tiny seed of madness took hold in my mind, setting me on a crash course with revenge.

"I saw..." I say. My voice is trembling so much that I can barely get the words out. "I saw you having sex with Tess on the kitchen island."

The darkness envelops us as we stand face to face, our eyes locked in a deadly duel. I crave for him to break the silence, to utter those three words that could make everything right again: "I am sorry." But he remains silent, his lips sealed tight, denying the apology I so deeply desire. The silence gnaws at my sanity, pushing me to the brink of madness.

Say something, Hudson. Say you're sorry.

I long for him to speak, to beg for forgiveness, but all I hear is the sound of my own frantic heartbeat echoing in my ears. The image of the two of them together burns bright in my brain, the shock and confusion of what I saw rushing back to me. I knew he was sleeping with Natalie, but to see him and Tess together was...unthinkable.

Finally, he blinks and takes in a long breath. His shoulders slump as he exhales, his body sinking into the chair.

"I didn't want to marry you, Vivian," he says.

What? I catch my breath, the words hitting me like a slap in the face.

"I knew it was a mistake the morning of our wedding," he continues. "I almost didn't go through with it but... If it wasn't for the pregnancy..."

He looks down at the ground and then raises his eyes at me again.

"After I found out you lied to me about the baby, that the pregnancy was a big sham, I was devastated. I flew out here to talk to Tess. I told her everything. I needed a friend. But she had a surprise for me. She confessed that she had been in love with me since college. I was caught off guard. Then she kissed me, started unbuttoning my shirt. I was vulnerable. It was easy to give in to her." His eyes go distant for a moment. He shakes his head again. "But I wasn't in love with her." He levels his eyes on mine.

"Just like I was never in love with you."

The contempt in his voice is unbearable. I stumble back into the darkness, my heart shattering into a million pieces. I had believed him, trusted him, loved him with every fiber of my being. Everything I believed about us was now crumbling beneath my feet. How could he lie to me so effortlessly? How could he make me doubt myself and my own reality? It was all so senseless, so cruel.

I try to reconcile his version of the truth with my own memories, but they don't match up. Hudson was in love with me, he had to have been. Was it all in my head? All the time we shared together... It was like trying to force together a puzzle where none of the pieces fit.

"You're lying," I say. My voice sounds small, fragile. "I know you loved me."

"Vivian, I'm telling you. If it wasn't for the pregnancy, I wouldn't have married you," he says. "Tess and I were only together a couple of times. The truth is, I'm in love with Natalie."

My insides begin to boil, churning with anger. "Let me get this straight. You claim to love Natalie while also sleeping with your college best friend? How many people can you juggle in your bed at once?" I shake my head slowly, my eyes narrowing in disbelief. "This whole story of yours is a big line of crap. The truth is you're a sex addict who can't keep it in his pants. And there's no one you could love more than yourself."

He lets out a puff of air, his face filled with anger.

"Whatever, Vivian. You're crazy, just like your mother."

Fury consumes me. Without thinking, I lunge forward

and strike him across the face with all the strength in my body. The impact is like a gunshot, his head whipping to the side as a searing heat spreads through my palm.

But it's worth it when I see the rage burning in his eyes, so dark and piercing that it sends shivers down my spine. He glares at me with pure hatred, and I know that I've hit my mark perfectly.

I stare at him in the dark, panting from the effort. He slowly turns his head from side to side, cranking his jaw back into place from the blow.

"Whatever it is you want, Vivian, let's get it over with," he says.

I let out a laugh. "Oh, it won't be that easy. Because what I have in store for you and that little bimbo out there is something that won't be over in one night. It's something that will be with you for the rest of your life."

He looks at me in the darkness, the anger on his face slowly turning into fear.

39

NATALIE

Three... Two... One... Jump.

After taking a final deep breath, I leap through the air and plunge into the dark water below. My life jacket keeps me afloat, but the choppy waves crash over my head. The pain in my arm shoots through my body like an electric shock, radiating from my wrist to my heart. Any movement of my arms causes a sharp pain as I struggle to move forward.

I frantically blink my eyes, trying to clear the mixture of rain and lake water. All around me is a blur of darkness, with only tiny lights on a distant shoreline providing any sense of direction. I whip my head around, desperately searching for my destination: the island, which seems farther away than when I jumped in. Another wave crashes over me and I'm pushed underwater, struggling to keep from drowning in the icy depths.

As I resurface, gasping for breath, I attempt to swim towards the island using only my dominant arm. But the wound on my left arm catches on my clothes, making it feel like I'm swimming through quicksand. Each stroke takes all of my strength and still I can only move a few feet. Panic sets in as I realize how far I still have to go and how weak I am becoming. But I can't give up, not yet. With every ounce of determination, I push through the freezing water and continue on towards the house on the hill.

I thrash my limbs desperately in the water, pushing towards the dock with all my strength. But as I struggle, dark thoughts flood my mind. All my hard work and determination to become independent, to pull myself up by my own bootstraps and make a life for myself, now feels futile.

In just one weekend, it seems like I've lost everything. All the money I've worked hard to save—$500,000—is now gone. Not only that, but I also owe a significant amount of money to the bank, and I have no means of paying it back. The thought of declaring bankruptcy or facing time in jail feels equally unbearable at this point.

And now? My boyfriend, the man I thought I knew and loved, has been deceiving me from the beginning. He was already married when we met, when we started dating, when we slept together. It's not just his actions that he lied about, it's his entire identity.

I used to pride myself on having good intuition and being able to see through people's facades, but clearly I was mistaken. The weight of my mistakes crushes me, pressing down on my chest and constricting my breath.

For a moment I feel like giving up. I think about unstrapping the buckles on the life vest and just drifting into the water. No one would really miss me. A few friends from work and maybe my assistant Claire. But even her, I've only known for a few months.

So I have no real friends, no family...and my boyfriend

has turned out to be a pathological liar. I'm completely alone.

What is it that I have to live for?

My body bobs like a lifeless doll in the cold, murky water, drenched in a mix of lake water, salty tears, and rain. Each breath feels like shards of glass piercing my lungs as I struggle to keep my head above water. As I gasp for air, the question echoes relentlessly through my mind, bouncing off every corner with mocking laughter. *What do I have to live for?* The answer evades me, slipping through my fingers like the water that threatens to swallow me whole.

It is the strangest memory that hits me in that moment. My first closing. I was so eager, so green. I had just started at the firm and was assigned my first clients. I wanted to make an impression, to show them how grateful I was for their business. So I showed up at the closing with coffee and donuts, enough for everyone in the office. It took me three trips to lug in all the coffee and two dozen donuts. The receptionist looked at me like I was the strangest creature she had ever seen, but my clients were delighted.

As we sat around the conference table, signing papers and exchanging pleasantries, I couldn't help but feel a sense of hope and excitement. This was the beginning of a new life for me. I had nothing to lose, really, and everything to gain. My clients were happy, the deal was going smoothly, and I was on top of the world.

Could I start over again?

Hanging on to that small thread of hope, I start kicking my legs again. Lying on my back, I lift my right arm and take that first stroke, and then another, and another. It seems my luck may have turned because the waves that are rolling across the lake seem to be going in the direction of the island. I have to stop every few minutes to catch my breath, but I keep going.

Eventually, after what feels like an eternity, I make it to shore.

I'm too weak to pull myself up on the docks themselves, so I let the waves carry me all the way to the stone seawall that surrounds the island. I rake my fingers across the surface of the stones and heave my body out of the water.

My lungs are burning from the effort. It's all I can do to keep my eyes open. The rain is still washing down on me while thunder crashes in the distance. I look up at the house and once again think of Hudson.

Is he waiting inside?

I know I can never be with him again after what happened but I could really use some of his helpfulness right now. Breathing suddenly becomes more difficult. A single word clings to my tongue.

Help.

I open up my mouth to form it, but it never comes out.

I know I need to make it back to the house but I suddenly feel the need to close my eyes, if just for a minute. And when I do, despite the thunder rumbling the ground beneath me, I let out a last breath and everything goes black.

40

VIVIAN

The memory of finding Hudson and Tess together that day still haunts me. The sheer horror and betrayal cut deep into my core as I stood frozen, watching them through the window, unable to move or even think straight. Somehow, I found the strength to gather myself and walk around the house, pressing my back against the walls to steady my shaking body.

After a few moments of collecting myself outside, I calmed down enough to sneak down the hill and into the boathouse. I decided to stay there until Hudson was gone, catching my breath in the process.

After two agonizing hours, I finally spotted him descending the path towards the boat dock. I crouched in the shadows, my heart pounding as I watched them kiss passionately before he boarded the boat taxi and disappeared into the horizon. I waited for what felt like an eternity, making sure he wasn't returning and that Tess didn't suspect anything.

The day was idyllic—sunny with a few billowing clouds

in the sky—a stark contrast to the turmoil boiling inside me. It was an unexpected burst of warmth in the midst of October, known as a second summer, but to me it felt like a cruel mockery of what I was feeling.

I made my way up to the house and, sure enough, Tess was surprised to see me at the door. I studied her heart-shaped face, looked deep into her bright green eyes, trying to find any clue of her betrayal. Anything that would suggest that just a few hours ago she was making love to my husband in the kitchen of this house.

But she revealed nothing. It was as if it never happened and I'd made the whole thing up in my head. But I didn't. I saw them clear as day. How could she do it? Betray me like that? Sleep with Hudson, when she knew we were still married. My entire plan for the weekend quickly unraveled. I knew I could no longer trust her to spread the news that Hudson was a liar and a cheat. She was just as bad as he was, if not worse. Not only was I losing my husband, but now I was losing a friend whom I'd known and trusted for years.

Another fragile thread of sanity seemed to unravel. I suddenly felt alone, like everyone was against me. But I didn't want to be the victim, have everyone feel sorry for me. No, that's not who I am. I wanted something more satisfying —justice.

I suggested we pack up a light lunch and the two of us took the small fishing boat for a cruise around the island. Tess seemed delighted by the idea. She even commented on how perfect a day it was for a picnic. Again, I was taken aback by the fact that just a few hours earlier she was screwing my husband on the kitchen island, and now she was ready for a picnic.

Her nonchalant attitude made it so much easier for what I had to do next.

As we glided towards the center of the lake, there wasn't a single boat in sight, leaving us truly alone on the vintage wooden vessel. Before leaving work for the day, one of the housekeepers from the estate had packed us an assortment of freshly made sandwiches, fruits, cheeses, and a bottle of white wine. I eagerly offered to carry the basket from the kitchen, secretly slipping a sharp knife inside as we made our way to the boat. The house help was leaving for the rest of the day, making the timing of our picnic perfect.

The water was eerily calm, no need for us to drop anchor. We simply drifted across the surface silently. The details of what happened next are a bit hazy for me. We exchanged small talk for about ten minutes, but I couldn't shake my growing nerves. My palms were sweaty and my eyes kept darting to the knife hidden inside the basket next to me. At one point, Tess went to the front of the boat to retrieve a bottle opener for our chilled pinot grigio. It was then that I reached into the basket and grabbed the knife, quickly tucking it back into one of the seat cushions, waiting for the perfect moment to use it.

As she walked back to where I was sitting, my heart pounded in my chest. I had so many questions...the biggest one of all being *why?* Why did she have to sleep with my husband when she could have anyone else?

I couldn't bring myself to tell her the ugly truth that I had witnessed that morning. Instead, I gave her one last chance to come clean and redeem herself. I asked her if she had seen or spoken to Hudson lately. Her answer? *No.*

It was that simple word that sent me over the edge. She kept talking, telling me lie after lie. *I haven't seen Hudson for months. I hope you two are doing okay. You're not? Oh, I hope you can work things out.*

Her lies where so deliberate, so flagrant that I thought I might become physically sick. By some miracle, I managed to keep my lunch down. A few moments later, she leaned forward to pluck a grape from the bunch arranged on our serving tray. I stood up, leaned forward and punched the knife right into her heart.

She struggled to speak, tried to call out for help, but her throat was obviously tight with fear. Blood seeped from the wound in her chest as she collapsed onto the deck of the boat. In that moment, I expected to feel something—panic, guilt, remorse. Yet all I felt was a detached sense of observation, like watching a scene from a movie. Without hesitation, I covered her body with a blanket. I steered the boat back to shore, my mind numb and disconnected from what I'd done.

I didn't want to kill again. Not because I couldn't. It was surprisingly effortless to end a person's life—too effortless. The lack of remorse I felt was almost unsettling. I was worried about the risk. Getting caught. And so that's when I came up with a plan.

I stare across the dining room, returning my thoughts to the present. That plan is about to become reality. I take a deep breath.

"After you left here a year ago, I stayed. I stayed and surprised Tess," I say, staring straight into Hudson's eyes. "I pretended not to have seen the two of you earlier, and of course she didn't mention it either. I suggested we take a little boat cruise and have a picnic on the water."

Hudson's looking at me now, his eyes growing wide with fear.

"Some people may call it an act of revenge. Or just pure

rage." I enjoy watching him squirm as I continue. "But let's just say when I plunged the knife into Tess's heart, it didn't hurt any more than when she stabbed me in the back."

Hudson's hands are frantically pulling at the ties that bind him, sweat trickling down his forehead as he struggles to free himself, the revelation of what happened to Tess washing over him and his animal desire to escape taking over. His eyes dart back and forth in desperation.

"Vivian, you have to let me out of here now. Listen, I'll go with you to the police. We can explain to them it was an accident," he says.

"An accident? Oh no, Hudson, this was no accident. It was murder, plain and simple. Which is exactly what the police are going to find when they go over the evidence."

Hudson's eyes shoot up at me. "What evidence?"

"This evidence," I say holding up two plastic bags, the objects inside knocking against each other as they sway in my gloved hands.

"The evidence that says you killed Tess McDermott."

He lets out a disdainful snort. "That's insane, Vivian. I didn't kill Tess. No one will believe you."

"Do you really think that? You forget that I'm a lawyer, Hudson. I know how a murder trial works. You had a motive, opportunity. And now I have two pretty convincing pieces of evidence." I dangle the first bag in front of him.

"This is Tess's cell phone. Full of text messages between the two of you. Proof that you were here that day and that you were having an affair." I hold up the second bag. "And this? The knife that killed Tess, covered in her blood. While you were snoozing on the kitchen floor, I made sure to get some of your nice, full-size fingerprints on the handle."

I can see the wheels are really turning now. He's scrambling, trying to come up with an idea of how to get himself out of this. But he won't because I have had a lot more time to think this through than he has. I gear up for the final blow.

"And to tie everything up for the judge in a nice little bow, I also have an eyewitness who can place you here the day of the murder. Motive, means, and opportunity. Not to mention bribery. I didn't know you had it in you, babe," I say, my words dripping with hatred.

Hudson's face is completely colorless now, almost green. His eyes are bulging.

"Yes, I know you paid off Bart to lie to the police and tell them you were never here. He confessed that little tidbit to me out of guilt." I tip my shoulders. "So, not only do I have some pretty tight evidence, but someone to corroborate my story too."

"You can't have a murder without a body, Vivian."

"The body? Oh, don't worry about that." A twisted grin spreads across my face and I release any remaining shred of sanity within me. It feels freeing to unleash everything, to no longer hold back. "I have the body too. In fact, I've already made an anonymous call to the police and they should be on their way. To find you trying to hide evidence of a murder."

Hudson is speechless now, staring at me in the dark. I can see that all the color has drained from his face and he's trying to decide what the heck he's going to do next.

"Now, you hang tight here, my dear husband." I reach forward and pat his cheek. "I've got to go put these back where they belong."

41

NATALIE

It's a clap of thunder that wakes me. A lightning bolt comes down from the sky and hits the ground what feels like right next to my body. I force my eyes open and inhale sharply, choking on the sudden intake of air. My body convulses, and I vomit lake water onto the wet ground. After wiping my eyes, I try to take stock of my surroundings as best I can.

I seem to have made it halfway up the rock embankment on the edge of the island. I push my body into a sitting position, which causes me to cry out in pain. Glancing down, I see that my left sleeve is now saturated with blood. I must've ripped open the stitches while I was trying to swim back.

So much for Hudson's handiwork.

With trembling hands, I fumble around my life vest and find the buckles keeping it closed. It takes all the strength I have to push the pieces of plastic together and release the clasp. The life jacket falls off my body, freeing me from what feels like a hundred extra pounds. I push the wet hair that's clinging to my forehead out of my face and take my first few stumbling steps towards the house.

The storm is still coming in waves, crashing down around me. I slip and slide up the wet grass of the hill, catching myself here and there with my good arm. By the time I've reached the edge of the house I am covered in mud. The front door will have locked behind me when I left, so I stumble around the house and end up near the back, where the kitchen is. I brush some more water from my eyes and see that there's actually a door at the rear of the property.

I need to get inside. Out of this storm.

I stumble forward and hit the ground once more. With determination, I pick myself up and struggle to get back on my feet. After much effort, I finally manage to reach the door and stand in front of it. My hand trembles as I grasp the large black iron handle. *Is it locked?* Pushing down with all my remaining strength, I feel a sense of relief as the latch clicks and the door slides open.

As soon as I detect the sound of voices, I stop in my tracks. The first voice belongs to Hudson and is instantly recognizable. The second voice is a woman's, and though it rings a bell, I can't quite place it. Hudson mentioned something about his ex-wife having tricked him here for revenge, and a sense of caution washes over me. I desperately want to reach Hudson and get help, but I stand by the doorway and listen intently. The voices appear to be coming from the dining room.

Seconds later, I hear heavy footsteps echoing towards the living room, their cadence indicating someone is leaving the room. A sharp click echoes through the air as the front door slams shut. My heart races as I take a deep breath and carefully peek around the corner of the dining room.

My breath hitches in my throat. My worst fears are confirmed as I see Hudson bound to a chair, his arms tightly secured to its frame with zip ties. Adrenaline pumping through my veins, I cautiously enter the room and move closer until I am standing directly before him.

"Natalie," he says, his eyes wide. His face is pale. He looks spooked. "Oh my gosh, are you all right? Did you fall in the water? What happened? You're covered in mud. Are you hurt? Your arm is bleeding..."

I'm at a loss for words in that moment, so I remain silent. Hudson struggles against the restraints binding his hands and feet and tries to move closer to me. I may be breathless, bleeding and covered in mud, but it suddenly feels like I'm not the one who needs help.

"I... I tried to take the boat. It was too choppy and I fell... I had to swim back," I manage, my eyes tracing over the ties on his body. "Why are you tied up?"

He's still struggling, trying to move his arms and legs. His face has a look of sheer panic.

"Natalie, you have to get me out of here. Go to the kitchen, find a knife or scissors or something and cut these ties."

Twenty-four hours ago, I would have done that without hesitation. But my mind instantly goes to the diary. The final words... Hudson killed me. Of course, if Tess is the one that bound Hudson to the dining chair, she's obviously not dead. But before I release him, I need more information.

"What's going on?"

He lets out a panicked breath. His eyes are wild with fear, mirroring my own. I've never seen him like this before.

"It's Vivian, my ex-wife. She's here on the island. She— ugh... She killed Tess McDermott. She admitted the whole thing to me. And..." He shivers. "She wants to pin the murder on me. She has Tess's cell phone and a knife. It's bad, Natalie, really bad. We've got to get out of here fast."

I study him for a few seconds, trying to decide what to do next. When I was walking up the hill, stumbling and falling in the mud, I had one singular thought in my mind. *Get to Hudson. He can help.*

Now that idea has been flipped on its head. He's sitting here, bound and tied. He needs my help. But the real question pounding inside my head is much more important.

Is Hudson lying to me?

Hudson sees my hesitation. "She's out for you too, Natalie. She wants revenge for our affair—"

"An affair I knew nothing about," I say, anger rising up inside of me.

"I know. I'm really sorry about that. I should have been honest with you from the beginning. But the situation with Vivian... It's complicated."

"You didn't have to lie," I say. My voice sounds small, almost childlike. Hudson's face softens.

"I am sorry, Nat. I really am. But I promise you if you trust me right now, I will get you off this island and home safe. We're in danger if we stay here. Vivian will be back any minute."

I chew the inside of my cheek, shift the weight on my feet. Hudson has been my rock, my confidant, my savior countless times. He helped me with the renovation of the flip house, and sewed up my arm after I tumbled down the rocks. Now, everything is different. I can't trust him like that again, not after what he's done. But as much as I want to push him away, I can't deny that he is my best chance at getting off this island. So, with a deep breath, I finally make a decision.

"I'll be right back," I say.

I trudge into the kitchen, looking for something to cut the zip ties with. The glint of a knife sitting on the counter catches my eye. I grab it and make my way back to the dining room, leaving behind a trail of water and mud.

"I found a knife," I say, holding up the blade in the dim light.

"Okay," he says, his voice breathless. "Hurry. Cut the zip ties on my hands first."

I kneel down and cut the ties around his wrists. Once his hands are free, I hand him the knife and he continues cutting the ties on his feet.

"They diary you told me about, where is it?"

I peer at him with a curious expression. "Why do you want the diary?"

"It's evidence that Vivian set this whole thing up. If the diary says I was married to Tess, it would be obvious that Tess didn't write it, because I was never married to her. So it's proof that Vivian is involved."

I nod, slowly beginning to understand. "It's in the blue room."

"Okay," he says, turning towards the staircase. "I'll run up and get it. You wait here."

"No!" I say, my voice louder than I intend. "We have to stay together. I can't—" My voice falters, and I have to hold back tears. *I can't be alone again.*

Hudson gives me a sympathetic nod. He places the knife in his left hand and wraps his right arm around my waist.

"Okay, we'll do this together."

We make our way to the stairs. I'm weak, but I manage to muster up enough strength to get up the steps and into the bedroom. The diary is lying on the bed, wrapped in the red scarf, just where I left it. I wait in the doorway while Hudson bounds into the room and snatches it up. He tucks the diary into his pants and hands me the scarf. I use it to wipe more water and mud from my face and then drape it across my neck.

"Come on," he says. "We're getting out of here."

A sudden thought occurs to me, sending a shiver down my spine.

"But the boat," I say, choking back tears. "I tried to take the boat and... It ran out of gas. I left it floating in the lake. It's probably long gone by now. I had to swim back." I shake my head weakly. "There's no way off the island."

Hudson places a hand on my shoulder. "It doesn't matter, Nat. The police are coming. We just have to make it outside." He gazes down the hall towards the stairs. "If Vivian finds us in here together I'm afraid she's going to kill us."

His words send a shiver down my spine. I lean into his body as we work our way through the hallway and down the stairs. When we arrive on the first-floor landing, I hear the front door swing open. My eyes snap to it.

We're too late. Hudson's ex-wife has already found us.

I brace myself against Hudson. He still has the knife in his hands. When I see the woman in the doorway, the blood in my veins turns to ice. At first I don't recognize her, then it dawns on me. It seems impossible, yet here she is.

"Claire," I say, my voice trembling. "What are you doing here?"

42

NATALIE

"Hello, Natalie," she says, her voice low and raspy. "It's good to see you again."

My heart stops as I lock eyes with her from across the room. I reach my hand to cover my mouth as my mind races, desperately trying to process the impossible sight before me.

It's Claire, unmistakably so, with those almond-shaped brown eyes and long, flowing auburn hair. But she is unrecognizable, her usually flawless face now streaked with smudged mascara and her neatly coiffed bun reduced to a mess of wet tendrils plastered to her skin.

But it's not her appearance that's throwing me off, it's the predatory gleam in her eyes. The Claire that I know, always with a smile on her face and eager to help, is gone. In her place stands a shell of a woman with vacant eyes and a posture like a predator ready to strike.

"I don't understand, Claire. What are you doing here?" I manage to choke out. She responds with a sinister cackle, sending shivers down my spine. Hudson's arms tighten around my waist, as if sensing the danger emanating from her.

"Oh, Natalie... You know, for someone who built a real estate empire all on their own, you're not very bright." An evil grin spreads across her face. "Don't you get it? Claire is only my middle name. My first name is Vivian. Vivian Claire Rockford."

Hudson's grip on me is the only thing keeping me from collapsing onto the floor.

"You see it now, don't you? I came to work for you as your faithful assistant, the dowdy little Claire. You pretty much handed me the keys to your kingdom on a silver platter. Financial documents, legal paperwork—it was almost too easy. But my favorite part was hearing the horror in your voice when you found out Declan skipped town with your entire life savings."

"You know Declan?"

A wicked smile spreads across her face. "Oh yes. You see, Declan is a friend of mine from law school. He owed me a favor...and, well, you know the rest of the story now."

My mind is reeling as everything finally clicks into place. Claire, the seemingly innocent woman who walked into my office six months ago, was actually a wolf in sheep's clothing. She has been handling all of my paperwork and files with ease, gaining my trust effortlessly. But now I see that it was all part of her grand plan to destroy me.

And Declan? I trusted him so easily. We had already done a couple of deals together, so when he asked me to front the money for the small apartment building, I eagerly agreed.

How could I have been so stupid?

I had been so consumed by my work, so blinded by my ambition, that I didn't see the warning signs. The subtle changes in her behavior, the look in her eyes anytime I mentioned Hudson. I just figured she was lonely, and therefore a little jealous of my relationship. It was why I always invited her out with us, tried to set her up on dates.

I was too focused on the success of my business, too determined to climb the corporate ladder to see what was happening right under my nose.

I stare at her, too stunned to speak.

"Vivian, you have to let us go. This has to stop now," says Hudson.

"That's exactly right, Hudson," she spat, her voice filled with venom. "This has to stop. Which is why you won't be free to run around and sleep with every woman you see any time in the near future. Once the police arrive and find what's been tucked away in the boathouse for the last year, you'll be spending the rest of your life behind bars."

Hudson's muscles tighten like steel cables around my waist. Vivian stands there, glaring at us in front of the slightly ajar door, her body outlined in the violent flashes of lightning. The storm rages on, waves of rain crashing against the building and piercing the gap in the front door.

Suddenly, a ferocious gust of wind lashes out, flinging the door open with a thunderous bang and nearly knocking Vivian off her feet. She uses her free arm to forcefully slam the door shut, shifting her focus away from us for a split second. Hudson lets go of me and rushes across the room, his knife poised to protect himself.

But Vivian is too fast for him. She pulls out a small handgun and points it at his face.

"Not so fast, my dear JJ," she says.

Hudson skids to a stop, raising his arms slightly.

"You wouldn't do it, Vivian. You don't have the guts."

"Maybe," she says, clicking the safety on the gun. "But how certain are you of that?"

Hudson takes a tentative step back. "You can't just shoot me in the face. What about your elaborate plan to send me to jail?"

Vivian cocks her head to the side but keeps the gun trained on his head.

"You're right, Hudson. I don't want to mess up that pretty face. Otherwise you won't be able to find a good boyfriend while you're rotting in jail."

With a sudden, unexpected motion, Vivian lowers the gun and takes aim at his leg. The sharp crack of the gunshot echoes off the walls, ringing loudly in my ears.

"Hudson!" I cry. I throw myself towards him as he stumbles backwards, our bodies crashing together. My arms wrap tightly around him, straining under his weight as we collide with the floor. The knife slips from Hudson's grasp and clatters noisily across the wooden planks beneath us.

Hudson writhes in agony, panting as he moans beside me. His hands clamp down on his leg, where the bullet has pierced through the skin, blood trickling out between his fingers. Panic rises in my chest as I frantically search for something to wrap around his leg.

"Hold on," I say, ripping off the scarf from my neck and tying it around his leg. The metallic scent of blood fills my nostrils, mingling with Hudson's labored breaths.

My eyes shoot up and I catch sight of Vivian approaching us. Her face is a distorted mix of emotions, the gun shaking in her right hand. I desperately try to pull Hudson away, but his weight proves too much for me. My muscles feel like they're on fire and my strength is quickly fading.

Vivian's finger curls around the trigger of the gun, her cold gaze fixed on the two of us. My heart slams against my ribcage, feeling like it might burst from the fear pulsing through my veins. Hudson lets out a low groan, as he tries to tighten the scarf around his leg.

"I don't want to shoot either of you again," she says, holding the gun firmly in one hand and extending her other hand towards us. "But I am going to need that diary."

"Fine," I say. I stand to a crouching position and reach over to pull the diary out of Hudson's waistband. "It's all yours."

I toss it across the floor in her direction. She bends down to pick it up, never taking her eyes off the two of us. Hudson isn't even watching her anymore, focused solely on his leg.

"Thank you," she says. She starts to back away towards the door. I stand up, a sudden rush of adrenaline hitting my veins.

"Why did you do it, Claire? Or Vivian, or whatever you name is," I ask, my voice cutting through the silence. "Why did you and Declan steal all of my money? I didn't know Hudson was married. I didn't know about any of this."

My voice is shaking, matching my trembling body.

Vivian reaches the door, her free hand fumbling behind her back, searching for the handle.

"Because I know he loves you. I can see it in the way he looks at you. And if I can't have Hudson, then no one can. I couldn't bear to watch the two of you live happily ever after."

The door handle clicks and she pushes down, cracking it open slightly. Just before she turns to leave, she gives me a menacing smile.

"I hope you enjoy bankruptcy, Natalie."

Her words dig into me, exposing an old wound that I thought had healed. A surge of energy, fueled by adrenaline or sheer willpower, propels me from my spot and across the room towards her. Her back is turn towards me now, slipping away into the opening.

I collide with her, using all my weight to knock her down. We crash to the floor. The gun flies out of her hand and skitters across the room. The door flings open and a gust of rain pours in from the raging storm. The floor is now slick beneath us, making it difficult to gain any leverage. We grapple and struggle, each trying to gain the upper hand.

I push harder, a primal instinct taking over. I will not let her hurt me again, not this time.

I frantically search the room looking for the gun. Vivian must be thinking the same because the two of us spot the gun at the same time. It's about three feet away from where Hudson is lying on the ground. I'm not sure he sees it, because he's still gripping his leg trying to tighten the scarf.

"Hudson," I cry out. "The gun!" He whips his head up, eyes searching wildly around him. He meets my gaze and follows it to the location of the gun. Vivian screams and tries to push my head into the floor. I smash my free hand into her face, and she falls away from me.

Both of us scramble towards the gun and Hudson, sliding across the floor.

But it's too late. Hudson has already reached the gun. He wraps his hand around it, points it towards her. At the same time, Vivian leaps up to a stand position. She reaches her arm out.

"Hudson, no!" she says.

I squeeze my eyes shut and hear another gunshot reverberate through the room. There is a loud thudding sound as her body drops to the floor. When I open my eyes, I see Vivian's lifeless body crumpled on the floor.

43

NATALIE

A few hours later as the sun begins to rise, casting a soft glow across the darkened sky, Hudson and I are huddled together in the back of the police boat, making our way to shore. The peaceful colors of pink and yellow slowly creep into the sky, signaling the start of a new day.

And for the first time in the last forty-eight hours, I feel a tiny bit of hope.

Exhaustion weighs heavily on my eyelids, causing them to droop despite my attempts to stay awake. The gentle hum of the motor and the rhythmic lap of waves against the boat are almost lulling me into a much-needed sleep. I can feel the heat of Hudson's body next to mine, but neither of us have said much since we left.

As we ride back to the mainland, I can't help but feel a sense of sadness and disappointment. The contrast between my excitement when we arrived on the island and my current state is stark. The trip has opened my eyes to the harsh realities of human nature, shattering my once naive *beliefs.*

I glance over at Hudson, who is staring at the shoreline, a distant look on his face. It's funny how in just a couple of days I learned more about who my boyfriend was than I did the entire year we were together.

When the paramedics and police arrived on the island, they quickly assessed his leg and stopped the bleeding. The bullet has only pierced the outer layer of fat on his thigh, resulting in a clean exit wound. They managed to stitch him up right there and then, but he is still in considerable pain. The light has yet to find its way back to his complexion, leaving him looking like a ghost caught between worlds.

I know that it's over between the two of us. The discovery of Hudson's deceit, not just towards me but also Vivian and possibly Tess, shattered any remaining trust I had for him. Throughout my life, I have learned that people rarely change, even if they try to convince us otherwise. It's difficult to believe that someone who consistently lies for their own gain is capable of reform.

And I deserve better.

I can't deny that I will never see Hudson the same way again, but a part of me is grateful to him for trying to save me from Vivian. The scar on my arm will serve as a constant reminder that people are capable of both good and bad actions. He deceived me, yet he also rescued me.

I let out a long sigh, watching as the sky continues to lighten around me.

I'm going to need a good therapist when I get back.

The police are checking us into a local hotel, so that we can shower and rest for a few hours before we head to the police station for more questions. I requested a separate room, of course. I am surprised they need to ask more questions. We have already spent hours speaking with them at the house.

It was just a few hours after the confrontation with Vivian that the police arrived. The storm had died down by then, but it was still freezing cold. Hudson and I sat in the dark house while we waited, going over everything that happened in detail. Enough so that when the police questioned us, we'd have our stories straight.

"So you didn't know about Tess? That Vivian killed her?" I remember asking him, my eyes searching his facial expression for any sign of a lie.

"No," he said with conviction. I had no choice but to believe him.

The police conducted an extensive investigation inside the house. After they arrived, one of the officers was able to figure out how to flip the power back on. The electrical panel had been tampered with, I'm guessing by Vivian herself. The house warmed up after that, and they made both of us coffee after the paramedics tended to our wounds. Honestly, I would've preferred the police station. It was hard to sit around the kitchen island Hudson and I had made love on a few days earlier and not think about the two of us together. Not to mention Vivian's dead body lying nearby in the foyer.

Vivian had mentioned to Hudson that Tess's body was hidden in the boathouse, but he had no clue where. It wasn't until the authorities showed up that we discovered its whereabouts. Apparently, Vivian had been hiding the body in a storage freezer within the garage beneath the boathouse. She had cleverly concealed it behind a false panel along the wall. Then, anonymously, she had informed the police about the exact whereabouts of the body.

I shift my position in the backseat, feeling Gucci's soft fur rustle against my legs. She stirs in my lap and I gently pat her head. When an officer came out of the boathouse with the carrier I made a quick decision to keep the cat. Hudson, not surprisingly, didn't want anything to do with her. The thought of leaving her alone on the island was unbearable to me, and besides, I could use some company at home. Her soft purr gives me a small bit of comfort.

I still haven't figured out how I'm going to get the money back from Declan. When Vivian revealed to us how she pretended to be my assistant and stole my life savings, Hudson was shocked. He hadn't known any of that was going on. When I explained to him what Declan looked like, it immediately rang a bell with him. His name was apparently John Declan Roberts, and it was true that he was a close friend of Vivian's from law school.

I didn't mention any of this to the police, knowing there wasn't much they could do. Even if it was fraud, a lawyer as shrewd as Declan would drag me through court for years trying to prove it.

Hudson has promised to do everything in his power to help me get the money back.

I hope it's enough.

The next few days pass by in a blur. Hudson and I each have a room at the Moose Lodge, and we make frequent trips to the police station to answer questions. I try to process everything that has happened. I find myself going through a range of emotions—anger, hurt, betrayal, and even a little bit of relief.

Hudson has been trying his best to make things right between us. He's been more attentive, constantly asking if I need anything and apologizing for what he did. And while

I appreciate his efforts, I'll never be able to trust him again.

But amidst all the chaos and confusion, I realize that there is a silver lining. The incident with the boat has made me realize how much I can truly rely on myself. When I was struggling to stay afloat in the water, when all hope seemed lost, it was my own strength and determination that kept me going.

I'm a survivor. No matter what life throws my way, I have the ability to overcome it.

44

THREE MONTHS LATER

"Hey, Gucci," I greet my cat as I set my keys down on the kitchen island in my apartment. Her white fur has grown long and fluffy and I enjoy her welcoming purr when I arrive home from work.

A few hours earlier, I officially closed the deal on a sprawling property nestled ten miles away. The structure is in desperate need of renovation, but I relish the challenge that lies ahead for the next few months. It feels good to be back in my element. My life following my return from Montana has been a little difficult at times, given everything that happened, but I've managed to come back on top, even financially.

About a week after I arrived home, Declan walked into my office. I was taken aback at first, wondering how he had the nerve to show up here unannounced. My immediate reaction was to call the police and press charges for everything he had done to me. And without a doubt, I could have easily done so.

But something stopped me. Maybe it was curiosity, or

maybe it was my desire to get my money back without having to involve the authorities—which I held out the most hope for. Either way, I decided to give him a chance to explain himself.

"Can we get lunch and talk?" he asked, his voice surprisingly calm and collected.

I hesitated for a moment before responding. I knew it would be a risk, but I also knew that I needed closure. And if I could get some answers, maybe I could finally put this all behind me.

"I owe you an explanation and an apology."

I glared at him. "And money," I spat.

"That too," he replied with a slight nod.

"Fine," I said, not quite sure if I meant it. About twenty minutes later, we were sitting across each other at an upscale restaurant down the road from my real estate office.

"I just can't tell you how sorry I am about all of this, Natalie," he says with a look of genuine remorse. "I am paying you back everything that we took, plus ten percent for your troubles."

I can't deny, in that moment I was a little bit excited to get my money back plus interest. A week ago I had been convinced that I was completely broke, and had been preparing to start from square one. But now, this unexpected stroke of luck had changed everything. It was as if the universe was rewarding me for my perseverance and determination.

"So, if you look in your bank account right now," he continued, "you'll see that the money is already there."

I swiped open my phone as John, aka Declan, watched me from across the table. The chatter and bustle of other diners filled the space behind us, punctuated by the clanking of dishes in the background. With a few taps on my phone, I confirmed what John had told me: the money was indeed in my account. A sense of relief washed over me.

But I still had questions.

"I just don't understand," I said, looking back up at him. He adjusted his tortoise-rim glasses and leaned forward.

"Understand what?"

"I don't understand why you did it. Why did you help Vivian even though you knew it was wrong?"

John let out a sigh, shaking his head. I could tell there was something else that he wanted to say but he held back.

"Vivian and I had a long history, starting back in law school. All I can tell you is that a few years ago she did me a favor. And if it wasn't for her, I wouldn't be sitting here with you right now." He suddenly looked as if he might start crying. "I can't lie to you and tell you I didn't love her. I miss her dearly right now. But after what happened I was afraid that she would never stop asking for favors." He shook his head. "That she would never stop seeking revenge."

I didn't press any further. To be honest, I was exhausted by all this drama. I didn't want to know anything else. I just wanted to go back to my job and continue my life just as it was before Hudson and I ever met.

I thanked John for making things right, and that was the last time I saw him.

After what transpired in Montana I was determined to prove to myself that I could start over again, even if it meant starting over from scratch. But I didn't have to. The whole experience taught me what I was really made of. And I planned on using this newfound confidence to take on bigger projects, further my burgeoning empire.

As far as Hudson goes? Well, I haven't heard from him in

a couple of months. And I prefer it that way. I was grateful that he did the right thing and protected me from Vivian while we were on the island, but of course, there is no way I could ever trust him again.

There was no formal investigation into his involvement in Tess's disappearance. After everything we shared with the police, it was clear that Vivian was responsible for her death. The diary ended up being a key piece of evidence in our story. They had a handwriting specialist come in and confirm that the diary was indeed written by Vivian herself.

It saddens me that Tess died the way she did, and even though there is no love lost for Hudson, I'm glad that he didn't go to jail for a murder he didn't commit. Perhaps losing two women he cared for was punishment enough. I hope whatever unsuspecting woman crosses his path in the future, he'll make better decisions.

Perhaps for once, he will make an effort to tell the truth.

Gucci purrs against my feet and I reach into the pantry and pull out a can of her favorite cat food. She weaves her way through my legs. I never imagined myself owning a cat but it's actually been nice. She keeps me company around the house. Even though she is a constant reminder of what happened in Montana, she's also a reminder of the strength that took to get through that situation.

I leave Gucci to nibble on her dinner and head to the bathroom to hop in the shower.

After three months, I think it's been enough time. I've decided to put myself out there and go on a date. The guy is a friend of a friend and works as an accountant at a firm in downtown Atlanta. And he has no travel schedule whatsoever.

Even though he seems like a perfectly normal sweet guy,

I ran a background check on him just to be certain. After what happened with Hudson, I decided to take matters into my own hands in the future. To my relief, it came back free and clear of any suspicious activity. Of course, that doesn't make him completely trustworthy, but it's a start.

If there's one thing I've learned from this whole experience, it's that people aren't always honest about who they really are.

EPILOGUE
JOHN DECLAN ROBERTS

I gaze out the window of my office, watching as the long streaks of rainwater wash down the large window. The Chicago skyline is lying beneath murky and gray skies today. I've just returned to the office following a court hearing and have about thirty minutes before I need to head to lunch. It's in these moments when things are quiet and no one is ringing my phone that grief really hits me.

I miss her.

Even though Vivian wasn't perfect in many ways, she was still someone I loved. After everything that happened in Montana I hung out at the Moose Lodge for a few days, just to see if she would return. But Flathead Lake is a small community and it didn't take too long before the rumors started to float their way around to the hotel. Tess McDermott's body had been found. And of course, the juiciest part of the gossip was that she had been murdered by her friend Vivian Rockford.

As for Vivian? She had been shot dead on the property

following a mysterious struggle with a young couple who was staying on the island. It didn't take me long to put two and two together. I knew exactly what had happened. I'd warned Vivian over and over again. I'd told her she was going too far but she just wouldn't listen.

My heart was shattered when I found out. Vivian had finally gone too far, and it had cost her her life.

I flew back to Chicago and waited for things to die down. I knew the best way to cover my ass in the situation was to come clean with Natalie and give her all the money back. The bank loan that Vivian had threatened her with actually never existed. It was just a bunch of forged documents that Vivian had created to torture Natalie.

I met with Natalie and told her the truth about everything. Except for one thing: what happened in Paris.

But it would lighten my heart if I came clean about it now. So here it is.

A few years ago, after Vivian and I passed the bar exam, we decided to take a sabbatical to Europe for a month. We started off in Ibiza, partying like we were twenty-one all over again. At the end of every night, I hoped that Vivian would come back to our place, confess to me that she felt the same way about me that I did about her. But she always seemed to find some attractive French or Spanish man to entertain her.

After a couple of weeks of the wild Ibiza lifestyle— endless clubbing, loud music, and drugs—we were exhausted. We hopped on a plane to Paris, planning to use it as our home base for the rest of our trip. The nightlife there was unrivaled and there was no shortage of attractive men and women to add to our indulgent experience before we had to return to reality and our demanding law firm jobs.

In a dimly lit club, I met an enchanting woman named Camille. We were instantly enthralled with each other and I eagerly invited her back to our penthouse suite at the hotel. Vivian wanted to continue partying at the club, so she stayed. But Camille had a different plan in mind. She pulled out some recreational drugs and we indulged, but to my shock, Camille couldn't get enough. Despite her tiny frame, she downed alcohol and drugs without batting an eye.

After we had sex, an act which I can barely remember, Camille suddenly became irrational. She jumped up from the bed, completely naked, and headed to the door. She said she had to leave. I grabbed her shoulder to stop her, and in doing so, knocked her to the ground. As she was falling, she hit her head on the corner of a marble dresser. The crack was so loud it echoed in the room. I stood over her, my alcohol-addled brain trying to work out what to do next. Blood was oozing from her skull, soaking into the hotel carpet. I ran to the bathroom and grabbed some white towels, tried to stop the bleeding. I'm really not good with blood and it was making me woozy. A few minutes later I passed out cold.

When I woke up the next morning, I found Camille lying on the floor surrounded by bloody towels like a macabre halo. It was clear that she was dead. Still overwhelmed, with a hangover and in shock, I called Vivian and told her what happened.

She told me to stay calm, and within fifteen minutes she was dressed and in my room. She told me exactly what to do. She had a connection with the consulate. He knew the right people that could get us out of the country quickly before anything happened.

Long story short, Vivian was the one who got me out of

trouble and saved me from spending the next twenty years in a French prison.

So when she called me from Montana a year ago and told me that she had killed Tess, there was nothing I could do but help her hide the body.

ABOUT THE AUTHOR

Leah Cupps is a Multiple-Award Winning Author and Entrepreneur. She writes Thriller, Mystery, and Suspense as well as Middle-Grade Mystery Adventure Books.

Leah's novels are fast-paced thrillers that will keep you up at night as you can't wait to see what happens in the next chapter.

Leah lives in Indiana with her husband and three children. When she isn't losing sleep writing her next novel or scaling her next business, she enjoys reading, riding horses, working out, and spending time with her family.

Did you enjoy *You Are Not Alone*? Please consider leaving a review on Amazon to help other readers discover the book.

Visit Leah Cupps on her website: www.leahcupps.com

ALSO BY LEAH CUPPS

One Last Bite

You Are Not Alone

Made in the USA
Las Vegas, NV
10 August 2024

93642143R00159